SURVIVORS

MARSHALL MILLER

BLUE FORGE PRESS
Port Orchard, Washington

Survivors
Copyright 2018, 2023
by Marshall Miller

First eBook Edition December 2019
First Print Edition December 2019
Second eBook Edition April 2022
Second Print Edition April 2022

Interior design by Brianne DiMarco
Cover art and design by Brianne DiMarco

ISBN 978-1-59092-972-8

For information about film, reprint or other subsidiary rights, contact: blueforgegroup@gmail.com

Blue Forge Press is the print division of the volunteer-run, federal 501(c)3 nonprofit company, Blue Forge Group, founded in 1989 and dedicated to bringing light to the shadows and voice to the silence. We strive to empower storytellers across all walks of life with our four divisions: Blue Forge Press, Blue Forge Films, Blue Forge Gaming, and Blue Forge Records. Find out more at www.BlueForgeGroup.org

Blue Forge Press
7419 Ebbert Drive Southeast
Port Orchard, Washington 98367
blueforgepress@gmail.com
360-550-2071 ph.txt

MORE BY THE AUTHOR

SPECIAL AGENT KIM KUPAR

Jade Eyes
They
The Why Files

THE TSCHAAA INFESTATION

Book 1: The Gathering Storm
Book 2: The Tsunami
Book 3: Typhoon of Steel
Free Range Protocol: Tales of the Tschaaa
Beyond the Great Compromise: Tales of the Tschaaa
Survivors: Escaping the Tschaaa

ANTHOLOGIES

Monstrosity (Unnerving Anthology)
Descent (Unnerving Anthology)
Wicked (Unnerving Anthology)
Nightfall (Unnerving Anthology)
The Mighty Pen
Unconditional
Cascadia
Tales of the Slug
Super: Unexpected Heroes Arise

COLLECTED WORKS & MORE

Inhumanity: A Year of Stories
The Island (The Haunting of Orchard House)
Shane (Angels of Anarchy)

DEDICATION

I would like to once again dedicate this book to my loving wife, Sheri, and our four-legged furry family for putting up with my late-night forays in creating weird and wonderful worlds from my imagination.

I would also like to dedicate this literary work of fiction to all real-world survivors. To all the survivors of war, abuse, disease, and disasters—both man-made and natural—remember one salient fact.

Where there is life, there is hope.

ACKNOWLEDGEMENTS

This novel is another adventure in the series my publisher and I have named *The Tschaaa Infestation*. Without my publisher, Blue Forge Press, this book delving into the experiences of young adults trying to survive during the early stages of the Tschaaa invasion would not exist. I give my heartfelt thanks for the support only an excellent publisher can give.

I also wish to acknowledge, once again, former Marine Greg Breshears, my friend and advisor in all things Corps related. He helps me keep the "Oorah!" in my action scenes.

Finally, to all my fellow authors and writers, especially all the members of Kitsap Literary Authors and Writers group, I extend my thanks in keeping me motivated to write that next story and beyond.

The Tschaaa Infestation has only just begun.

SURVIVORS

MARSHALL MILLER

I

It was a typical late summer Western Washington Day in the neighborhood. The sun still climbed in the early morning sky before a Pacific Northwest autumn. The houses off of Shaw Road in Puyallup sat on a hill that looked down on the city proper if trees were not in the way. A 'higher end' neighborhood both in elevation and real estate prices, the residences in the culdesac were large two and three car garage structures designed for upper class and upper mobile families. Even so, the homeowners still had the typical problems of any suburban residents.

This morning Mrs. Deeds once again chased her small Chihuahua dog Pedro down the street, screaming at him to return as Pedro chased the neighbor cat Snowball. The question among the residents knowledgeable of this daily occurrence was what would happen if Pedro ever caught Snowball. There was even a private betting pool as to the outcome. Most of the of the money was on Snowball.

Mr. Folsom grumbled as he once again had to look for his morning paper in the side bushes of his home. He swore to himself for the umpteenth time that he would cancel the newspaper due to poor service. However, he never did.

And in the Richards house, there emanated the sounds of the early morning activity of a family with two working parents and two teenage children. Sounds of hurried breakfast preparation mixed with the sounds of two adults attempting to find keys and briefcases. In a room, the second floor, a loud, raucous noise (which the occupant of the room claimed was "modern music") blasted out past the closed door. From under a puffy pink quilt, a feminine hand snaked out. The hand attempted to smack the clock radio into silence while at the same time keeping the head of the hand's owner concealed under the bed covers. Finally, the hand found its target and sent it smashing to the carpeted floor. There was a squealing noise, then silence.

"Sister, did you break another clock?" a young male voice called through the closed door as the teenager lightly knocked.

"*Go away!*" A yelled answer was muffled by the bed covers and quilt. "Just ten more minutes…"

A couple of minutes later, there was a louder knocking on the young ladies door. The voice which had the tone of a mother frustrated once again with a late rising teen called through the door.

"Janice! Get up if you want to get a ride from your Father. You said you wanted to make that early morning extracurricular activities meeting."

Janice groaned. Why did morning come so early?

"Janice!"

"Alright, Mom! Geesh. I'm up."

Not for the first time did Jean Richards have a fleeting wish she had given birth to two boys rather than a girl and a boy.

Her husband Jack said that Janice was too much like her mother with an aggressive and stubborn streak a mile wide. It did not keep Jean from seething at the comment when Jack added: "But that is what makes you so loveable, Babe."

Blonde and still shapely Jean moved about the kitchen making some breakfast as Jack stood over the table top counter that acted as a small table in the kitchen area. He was eating his daily Breakfast of Champions; Wheaties with a few raisins and "rat poison" (artificial sweetener) sprinkled on top, in a bowl of milk. Jean began to grumble to herself as she tried to fry some eggs.

"Honey," said her husband. "Don't let her get to you. If she's late for the activities meetings, that is her problem, not yours."

"Oh really?" Jean shot back. "Then we have to listen to her whine and grouse on end because she could not do such and such, be on this or that team."

"Jean, all teenagers complain…"

"And I for one am tired of hearing it, goddammit!"

"Mother. Language." The voice was from James, Jean's brother. As he spoke, he reached for the Curse Jar on the counter. "A dollar, Mother."

Jean stared at him, then spoke. "You want breakfast?"

"Yes, please," responded James.

"Then go upstairs and get your sister moving!"

"Yes, Mother." James set the jar down and went to comply with his mother's request.

James was different. He was a year older than his sister but had been held back a year, so they were now Juniors in high school together. Janice was sixteen going on twenty-five and James was seventeen going on—it was hard to tell. The Richards had taken James to every type of medical specialist imaginable to the couple. Jack's job in aerospace and Jean's oral surgeon practice gave the two excellent medical insurance. Aspergers, Autism, ADHD, ADD, static encephalopathy, mutated brain cells...they had heard them all. But the bottom line was, no one had an answer. One minute James was a savant, able to play on aria on some musical instrument with no lessons, the next he had trouble opening his door. Jack once said it was like he had an intermittent short circuit caused by a loose wire in the form of some neuron or two which flopped to and fro because of God knew what. The problem was the 'loose wire' could not be found. So, for weeks on end, no problems. Then, a day or two or weirdness. Like the time he began taking the clothes dryer apart in the middle of the night.

"James, what are you doing?" a sleepy-eyed Jack had asked.

"Seeing how it works, Father."

"Why, at three-thirty in the morning, Son?"

James had shrugged, then started putting it back together. Jack told Jean it was like he was receiving messages on a different wavelength than everyone else, from God knew where. The dryer worked perfectly after James' attention.

To say these intermittent but sometimes bizarre actions caused James some social problems was an understatement. An issue was they also created social problems for Janice, a teenager trying to dodge the landmines of mean girls, horny boys, and social clicks. No young lady advancing through puberty wanted to be tagged the one with the Weird Brother. She had gotten in some fights in her early years when someone had called James 'retarded.' Young ladies in upper suburbia did not brawl. Thus as she grew older, she became more frustrated with this situation. Nasty remarks about her flesh and blood reflected back on her. Maybe she was 'retarded' also, other kids would jeer.

James came back down the stairs with a grumpy Janice following.

"I told you I was coming," said Janice.

"Well, your father is not going to be late to work because of you. He offered to give you a ride to help you out, young lady," replied her mother. This was a conversation oft heard in numerous variations. Frustrated mother tried to get the daughter to do something, daughter pushes back, so mother persists, so daughter rebels... it soon becomes a constant circular argument and response.

"So, just gimme some toast, if everyone is in a hurry."

"Janice, did you not hear me? Your father is doing you a favor. At least show him some respect."

The two females glared at each other, a conflict as old as human society.

"Okay, everybody, let's have some toast! And blackberry jam." Jack did what he always did; jumped in to lighten things up, try to defuse arguments.

Jean harrumphed and finished the eggs, then shoved them unceremoniously onto a plate. She pushed them at the two children.

"You split these. I have to get to work also, remember?" Jean went to the master bedroom to finish her morning ritual. Janice looked as if she was on the verge of some sarcastic retort when she saw the look in her father's eyes and decided discretion was the better part of valor in the situation. James split the serving of scrambled eggs precisely in two, slid half on another plate and gave it to his sister. Janice wolfed them down as her brother concentrated on eating his in equal sized bites. Janice grabbed a glass of orange juice, took two gulps, then ran back up the stairs to her room to finish with her preparations for the school day.

Jack looked at his son as he ate in such a singleminded way and sighed. James looked like a younger version of Jack, brown hair and just above average height. There the similarity seemed to end. To be able to block out all the conflict around him was an ability Jack wished he had. He put his bowl in the sink, rinsed it, then claimed his suit coat and briefcase.

"Finish up, Son. Grab your stuff and I'll meet you and your sister in the SUV."

"Yes, Father."

As James and Janice exited their father's SUV at the school, Janice said: "Wait up a minute James." Her brother dutifully stopped.

"Look, James. Please do me a favor."

"Yes, Sister."

"If you see me with some people, can you kind of stay away? I'm trying to make some new friends this year, I need time alone with them. Okay?"

"Okay, Janice," James replied. He then did an about face and walked away without further comment.

"You act like a robot sometimes, James, " Janice mumbled to herself. "Do you realize that?" She looked around, saw a couple of girls talking to the Senior Captain of the High School Football Team. They waved her over, and she went with a smile.

"Frank, this is Janice," said the young Asian girl named Sumi. Tall and muscular Frank smiled at Janice.

"Hi," he said. "Was that your brother?"

"Hi, back. Yeah, that's James. One of the four 'Js' as my Dad says." Janice flipped her well brushed blonde hair just enough to draw attention to it.

"All your names start with J?" Frank asked. Janice noticed Frank had pretty deep blue eyes.

"Yeah. My Mom and Dad had a special sense of humor naming us."

"Her Brother is, 'special,'" the other girl, a brunette named Heather said with a wry smile. Janice glared at her.

"See you at lunch?" Frank asked.

"Hope so," Janice replied.

"Come on," Sumi said. "We're going to be late for the Special Activities Meetings. Do you want to try out for Cheerleader or what?"

Janice watched Frank walk away with a bit of young lust in her heart. Maybe this year would be alright after all.

Jack sat in the 'Waiting Zone' in front of the High School. He told the kids he would pick them up after school. It was on his way home from the well known aerospace company sub-office anyway, so it was no big deal. He signed as he drank his iced soda. September twelth and a decent sunny Washington Summer was still holding up. Another month and it would be rain and Washington Drool, that odd precipitation that one moment seemed a heavy mist, then the next a cold drizzle. He smiled to himself. Well, the way work was looking, he would be too busy to worry about the weather. Suddenly the Government and various major private 'Space Launch' companies were all vying to be the first to launch some kind of drone or operated craft at the humongous Asteroid 18666 which was passing uncomfortably close to the Earth. In fact, it was moving between the Earth and the Moon. All the Talking Heads on the various television channels were pointing fingers, demanding why no one seemed to realize the asteroid of that size would pass so close to humanity's home. A rumor started that its path had been disturbed early on its entry into the orbital plane of Earth. Which then started conspiracy chatter on the Web and late night radio. Was someone "directing" the celestial object!? He chuckled. Yeah, right.

Just then, the passenger side back door was jerked open. Janice climbed in and slammed the door, hard. Jack frowned as he looked in the rearview mirror. His daughter's face was flushed with rage.

"Ah, Honey?"

"I. Don't. Want. To. Talk." Jack thought she would start spitting nails any second as her face was so red with anger. Just then, James entered and sat in the 'shotgun seat.' He began to say something to Janice, and she cut him off.

"*Don't. Don't say a word.*"

Jack decided it would be best not to start an investigation as to what went wrong that minute.

"Put your seat belts on," he directed.

He managed to engage James in some small talk about Asteroid 18666.

"Uncle Mark called me in the office. Said he had some inside info from some of his military and Government sources." Jack's brother Mark had worked for some Alphabet Agencies over the years and kept some contacts which were 'spooky.'

"What did he say, Father?" James asked.

"That the huge rock should not have entered the Solar System, nor transited as it did. He said it may have been nudged by something... or someone."

" Did Uncle Mark work on the X-Files?"

Jack laughed.

"I think he believes he did."

Janice rode in stony silence.

When the trio arrived home, Janice bolted from the SUV, slammed the door, went straight to the house front door. She went in, slammed the door and stormed up the stairs to her room. Jean had gotten home just minutes prior and was in the bathroom freshening up. She heard the door slam, felt the stomping of someone up the stairs. She walked into the entranceway as Jack and James entered.

"What is going on, Jack?" Jean asked.

"I made her mad," James answered.

"How?"

"She was talking to a boy at lunch. I forgot she told me not to bother her and I sat down next to her. She said I ruined everything for her."

"What?" Jean asked. "How?"

James just shrugged. Jean looked up the stairs, then began to move towards them.

"Honey, how about you let her cool down a bit before..." Jack was talking to Jean's back as she walked up the stairs towards Janice's room. He looked at James.

"Come to the kitchen, James. Time for a snack."

Jean knocked on Janice's bedroom door.

"Honey, can I…"

"*Go away!*"

Jean had not heard Janice this angry in ages. Something awful must have happened.

"Janice, come on. We can talk about it.."

Her daughter stomped to her bedroom door and flung it open. "Talk about what? That I have a spastic brother, who chases people off because he is weird? That ruins my chances at being even a little bit popular? How about me having a normal life without everything being about him and his problems?" Jean had never seen her daughter so angry before. But she also did not like the way she was talking about James.

"Now look, honey. It's not James' fault. You know he—"

"I know whose fault this is! *Yours, Mother.*"

"What?!" Jean shot back.

"I heard you and Dad talking about how wild you were! All the drugs and booze before you settled down with Dad. You fucked up your body, so you gave birth to a fucked up kid! I was lucky I came out halfway normal. But now thanks to your fuck-ups, I have to live with a brother who scares people away because he is so weird. So, because of your nasty body, I—"

The slap sounded like a pistol shot. Jean struck her so hard that Janice stumbled back into her room. *"How dare you!"* Jean screamed.

Jack had started to make his way towards the stairs when he heard Janice's ranting. He heard the slap and began bounding up them.

"You hit me!" Janice yelled back.

"How dare you talk to me that way. And about your brother that way." Tears of rage and hurt streamed down Jean's face. "You don't like it here, *get out!*"

"Okay. I *will.*" Janice turned around and marched to her closet, tried to pull a luggage set form under some clothes.

"What happened?" Jack demanded.

"She hit me!" Janice yelled from the closet.

"Janice, why..."

"Don't you dare take her side! You should have heard what your daughter said about James and me."

"Janice, what...

"I told the truth! Your fucked up body—"

"Say that one more time, Janice!" Jean stepped towards her daughter.

"*Goddamn it!*" Jack bellowed, and everyone froze. Bellowing was so far out of his character that it was bizarre. "Everyone, shut up."

Mother and daughter glared at Jack and each other. Jack stepped in between them and held up his hands like a traffic cop.

"Okay. You're both mad. Great. But this is getting us nowhere."

"Father, I'm sorry." It was James. He had come up the stairs. "It's my fault. I can leave."

"No. Dammit." Jack stood for a moment. Then spoke. "It is what it is. It is no one's fault. 'Shit Happens' as the bumper sticker says. We are family, so we deal with problems together."

"Too late for that," Jean said. "I will not be blamed for James' problems or anybody's problems. Not after I worked my ass off through medical school and gave that little bitch a big house and everything she wants." Jean spun around and went quickly down the hallway and stairs.

" Janice—" Jack started to say, but she cut him off.

"Leave me alone." She turned and threw herself on her bed, began to cry.

Jack threw his hands up in frustration.

ean gave Jack the cold shoulder in bed that night, refused to talk about the festering open wound the nasty conflict between the two females in the family had opened. Jack arose earlier than usual as he could not sleep. He went down to the kitchen and made coffee early. Jack tiptoed out the front door and found the daily paper. He knew it was an anachronism but still liked to read a newspaper, no matter how thin, with his morning coffee. As Jack sipped his coffee, James entered the kitchen. His eyes were puffy with sleep, and his hair needed a comb.

"Can't sleep, James?" his father asked. The son shook his head.

"This will blow over, James. It just will take a while." James stood still. Then, slowly, he moved up and hugged his father.

"I'm sorry, Father."

"Sorry for what, James?"

"I forgot, bothered Janice, embarrassed her, made her

angry."

Jack gently broke James' embrace his son and looked at him. "Look at me, James. Everyone makes mistakes, forgets things. That does not excuse the reaction your sister had, nor how angry your mother became. You did not cause anything, This situation has been building for some time."

"I know, Father. I know they are frustrated. I wish I were... normal."

Jack did not know what to say. He could not really imagine what it was to be 'James.' Basic normal one minute, then a seemingly short circuit somewhere in his brain. Jack knew James 'saw' and felt things differently at various times in a given day. His son had tried to explain it once. All Jack could do was to try and not look befuddled.

"Son, we are who we are. And what is normal one day can be seen as different the next. Just be you, don't try and hurt people, or be mean, and you'll do just fine."

"Okay," replied James. But Jack could sense he was not okay

"Come on, Son. I'll make you some of that tea you like."
"Thanks, Father."
Jack and James had some 'guy' time for a good half hour, During that time, Father and Son talked about normal everyday things, like how James was doing in school the first week or so, was he thinking about College, a career? Jack never talked down to Jack, tried to tell him he was limited in his future. He wanted James to strive for everything he wanted. Otherwise, how would the young man know what he was capable of if he just lived to other peoples expectations?

Jean walked into the kitchen as the two males talked. James saw her, and said, "I'll turn on the News, Father," and walked into the connected large living room. Jack looked at Jean, saw her puffy face and red eyes.

"Can I get you some coffee, Honey?"

"Yeah," Jean mumbled back. She shuffled slowly to the

refrigerator and opened it. She stood staring at its contents as Jack walked up and hugged her.

"Rough night?" He asked.

"Yeah, the roughest." As Jean said that, she turned and hugged her husband, the love of her life since college. She began to sob softly into his shoulder. Jack held her as she cried, rubbed her back.

"We'll work this out, dearest. Okay?"

"I… don't know if we can, Jack. I feel so… broken. Maybe Janice is right. It is my fault."

Jack tilted Jean's face up towards his and answered. "Babe, we have been over this before. And all those doctors agreed. No one knows why Jack is the way he is. But that does not stop him from loving us, or us him." He gently kissed her.

"I love you, Aero Man," Jean replied with her personal nickname for the father of her children.

"And I love you, Tooth Fairy." They hugged each other again.

It was 6:18 AM Pacific Standard Time.

"Mother, Father, come look. Something happened in Atlanta."

"What?" Jack said, the private moment interrupted. Arms around each other, he and Jean walked into the living room and looked at the big screen television. The words of the newscaster began to register.

"This just in," the male eye candy said. "Just a few minutes ago, an object smashed into downtown Atlanta, Georgia. The first report is that it may be pieces of a crashing aircraft…" The young man with the coifed hair paused as someone babbled in his ear.

"Now officials are saying it is a piece of space debris, maybe a meteor."

"The asteroid, Father. Remember?" James said.

"Yes, Son. You may have hit it on the head. That asteroid, what was the number?"

"18666. You said Uncle Mark called you about it."

"What?" Jean asked with a confused frown on her face.

"Mark called, said he had some inside info about that object passing in Near Earth Orbit..." The newscaster interrupted his chain of thought with a rapid chatter.

"There's more of them! Reports are that objects, some say flaming rocks, are striking from coast to coast. The White House and FEMA have activated the nationwide Emergency Broadcast System..."

The widescreen television's picture flickered, then went blank. Seconds later, the EBS symbol appeared on the screen, followed by the irritating alert sound Jack usually heard on the radio.

"This is the activation of the Emergency Broadcast System..." the television went blank again. Static. Then nothing.

"James, get the emergency radio I gave you last Christmas."

"Yes, Father!" James shot up the stairs to his room.

"Jack, what is happening?" asked Jean

"That damned asteroid must have drug some space rocks with it. Idiot government people were too stupid to pay attention. Now some are entering our atmosphere, like stones from a slingshot."

"What can we do?" Asked Jean. "I have patients at the clinic today."

"Not now, Babe. Roads will be tied up as FEMA runs hither and yon—" Jack never had a chance to finish voicing his thought. There came an ever-increasing swooshing, crackling, humming sound that began to turn into a rumble. Jack's eyes widened, then he grabbed Jean.

"Down!" He pulled her to the carpet as something substantial in size whizzed over the house. Something made Jack start counting.

"One thousand one, one thousand two, one thousand three..."

There was a crashing boom that shook the house. Something had smashed into Puyallup.

"Father! I have the radio!" James yelled as Janice screamed from her bedroom.

"James! Get Janice!"

"What the hell was *that*?!" Jean asked from underneath his protective arms.

"Space rock smashing us. I counted about three seconds like with lightning and thunder. But that object was not traveling at the speed of light, so…"

"Here's Janice," proclaimed James as his sister scrambled over to join her parent on the floor. James remained standing, fiddling with his radio. It began to blare the same irritating EBS tone as from the now dead television.

"Son, get down, please?" Jean asked.

"Oh. Okay." He plunked down on the carpet. The radio finally began to broadcast an emergency message.

"There have been numerous meteor strikes across the United States. The State of Emergency has now been declared by the President of the United States traveling on Air Force One. He is landing at an undisclosed location due to further debris from Outer Space striking across the United States. People should stay in their home or shelter in place until further notice. Additional instructions from the President will be broadcast shortly."

The radio broadcast began again with the same irritating sound. "James, turn that off, please," said Jack. Everyone looked at him, their eyes asking 'Well?'

"We still have power, the lights are still on," said Jack. "James, Janice, get those bugout bags Uncle Mark made for you."

"Dad, why?" asked Janice. "The radio said to stay in place."

"Because, dear, if enough meteors hit, they may start residential fires that the local fire departments will not be able to handle. Like those large brush and forest fires in California. Whatever flew overhead, hit within a mile or so I bet."

"Meteorites, Father," interjected James. "After they hit, they are meteorites."

"Thank you Mister Wizard," Janice said sarcastically.

"Okay, no bickering. Janice, Jack, do what I tell you. We have to plan for the worst."

James jumped up to comply as Janice grumbled.

"Put some outdoor clothes on also. Jeans, jacket, decent shoes." Janice grumbled some more at her Father's commands.

"I'll make some breakfast before the power goes out," Jean said.

"Good idea. The satellite TV service might have been knocked out by the space debris. Get some more clothes on first. I'll grab our bugout bags." Jack kissed Jean and went to the bedroom. The bedroom window was open, and Jack thought he smelled smoke. He grabbed the bags of emergency supplies and strode to the front door. Jack set the bags down and went out on the front porch, looked and sniffed. He walked to the street sidewalk and from that vantage point could easily see the black plume of smoke he was smelling. It was roiling up in the sky from just over a mile away. Judging by the size of the plume, Jack thought a whole suburban block was on fire. That was not a good sign, although he heard sirens of approaching fire trucks. He turned to walk inside and thought he heard some noise from above.

The second rock seemed to come in at a steeper angle, as when Jack looked up, he thought it was coming straight down at him. He scrambled inside his home yelling for everyone to get down. He chanced a glance over his shoulder and thought he saw a smaller smoking object cross the horizon, heading beyond Puyallup.

"It's going to hit Joint Base Lewis-McChord." The thought flashed thru his mind as he ran to the kitchen to huddle with his wife and family. As the four humans huddled under the large dining room table of solid oak, there was swooshing, whistling, and crackling sounds as the house windows once again shook. Jack held his family as tight as he could, expecting them to be atomized any moment by a huge space object come to Earth. But, nothing happened.

"Father?" queried James.

"Must have got the angle wrong. I thought it was headed right for us."

The house then shook as a stupendous distant explosion rolled through the suburban neighborhood. Janice let loose with a scream as the shaking finally subsided. Then the power went out.

"Jean, see if the food on the stove is salvageable. You two kids stay put." Jack went out the back. Over the back fence, he saw a vast black cloud rising from the distance. Jack estimated this rock had struck close to two miles distance. Fire south of them spreading and fire to the west. Not good. As he thought that, he heard neighbors, now awake, coming out of their houses, shouting, crying out alarms as they saw the thick columns of smoke. Jack quickly re-entered the house.

"Janice, Jack. Put those bugout bags in my SUV. Then get the two coolers from the garage and bring them to the kitchen."

"Wait a minute," said Jean. "What are you doing?"

"We need to head to Uncle Mark's cabin up by Buck Creek near Darrington. If we head out now, keep to the back roads, we may dodge the gridlock…"

"Gridlock? What gridlock? There has been a meteor shower. The authorities will handle…"

"No. they will not. I have seen three good sized space rocks in the last five minutes. There are bound to be dozens more. Oversized ones could hit with the force of a tactical nuke. I learned about that when I was an Aircraft Engineer in the Air Force."

"Come on, Honey! That was years ago, just before you met me. You sure you remember right?"

"Jean, I'm not going to argue. This is going to be a national disaster. Things will fall apart real quick, and good neighbors may not be so good."

Jean's eyes widened a bit.

"What? You've been talking to your brother too much. He has your head filled with all that survivalist crap." Jack set his jaw, then walked over the cupboards. He reached up and grabbed some boxes of dry cereal and pasta, walked over and dumped them on the dining table. Jean stared at him as he walked back towards the cupboards.

"You're damned serious, aren't you?"

"Yes Jean, I am."

"Well, I'm staying here! I have patients with some pretty severe dental problems coming in the next couple of days. I'm not..."

"Jean, listen to me. This is not some winter storm that knocked out the power. This is like a super hurricane is blowing through Puget Sound..."

"Father! The radio!" James called out then walked into the kitchen with the radio blaring and Janice following.

"All citizens should expect to look to themselves and their neighbors for help," the voice on the radio stated. "Meteors are coming down all over the world, destroying the infrastructure primarily in the coastal areas. The national power grid is failing as major power stations, and power line systems collapse. People are advised to eat perishable food first as there is no question that power for refrigeration will be absent for weeks to a month. All power systems will be used to support medical..."

A shot rang out from the main street. Then two more. The Four J 's jumped and stared at each other. Jack broke the inertia when he dashed to the master bedroom.

"Mother, what is going on?" asked Janice. Before Jean

could answer, Jack strode by with a long-barreled pump shotgun in his hands.

"Jack!" Jean yelled, but Jack called back "Stay inside!" and continued out the front door. Before Jean could stop him, James was out the door behind his father. The two women looked at each other. They heard some loud voices, then the loud report of a twelve gauge shotgun.

"Jack," Jean called out as she ran to the front door. She stepped out onto the front porch and stopped. Laying in the street was Phil Dikes, a neighbor two doors down. Blood was pooling around the apparently dead man as there was brain matter mixed in with the blood. Farther down the street was Mike Jones. He was laying in the middle of the road holding his leg. A pistol was in the roadway just out of Mikes reach. The big shock was that Jack was pointing the shotgun at Mike as Daisy, Mike's wife, stood on the sidewalk screaming.

Mike Jones began to babble as his blood seeped through his fingers.

"That son of bitch Phil has been porking Daisy for weeks! I found out last night."

"So you picked this morning to shoot him?" Jack called out.

"We all came out in the street when the meteors came, and he walked up to Daisy…" Mike cried out as the pain hit him.

"Jack, we have to stop that bleeding," Jean tried to interject in a calming voice.

"I hit him with heavy game shot, not full buckshot," Jack answered. "I could've shot him in the head, and he'd be dead."

"Why did you shoot him at all?"

"Because he kept waving his pistol around, pointing it at Daisy."

Jean slowly walked over to Mike. Being an oral surgeon, she knew all about wounds and bleeding.

"Kick the pistol towards me, please," said Jack as if he were on some cop reality show. Instead, Jean carefully picked the handgun up with her hand well down on the butt away from the trigger. She kept the barrel pointed in a safe direction as she handed to Jack. Her dad had been a cop, so she had gun safety almost beat into her.

Mike had gone shooting with his brother Mark, who was a bit of a 'gun nut.' Thus, Mike saw the pistol was an automatic with a decocking lever to render the pistol 'safe' before he stuck it in his belt. Daisy kept bawling, looking from one person laying in the street to another as Jean a look at her husband's wound.

"Mike, instead of pointing the shotgun, can you go in and get that EMT bag I have stashed? I'll try to tend to this wound as best I can. Until the cops show up."

"Don't hold your breath," responded Jack. He went in and found the requested EMT bag. James and Janice had been peaking out the front window to see the action.

"Kids, get the coolers, start filling them up as I said."

"But Dad, Mom said..." Janice began to opine, but Jack cut her off.

"I'll talk with Mom. Just do what I said. Now." Janice grumbled as she went with James to fill the coolers. Jack took the EMT bag to his wife. All the other neighbors were now hiding in their homes, other than one couple who was on vacation and Phil's wife, now visiting a Daughter who had just given birth. Jack momentarily thought she would be a Widow if she ever made it back to Puyallup.

Jack watched his wife matter a fact way of bandaging Mikes wound after picking the Number 7 shot out of his leg as best she could.

"There. That ought to hold until you see a doctor," Jean said. She looked at Jack. "Can you help get him to his house, Jack?"

Five minutes later, with a sobbing Daisy hovering over him, they had him on his couch.

"I guess I'll be arrested," Mike said.

"I doubt it," grunted Jack. "The Police have bigger fish to fry right now with probably mass casualties." He looked at Jean. "Come on. We need to take care of our own."

As the two walked back to their home, saw the dark smoke clouds climbing ever higher, Jean spoke.

"I thought you gave the shotgun back to your brother.'

"I stashed it in my golf bag," said Jack.

"You know I don't like guns around James."

"Why, Jean? You know he has never shown anybody any violent behavior."

"What if he tried to take a gun apart like the dryer?" retorted Jean.

"He knows better than screw with my golf clubs. If you expect more out of him, you'll get more. With rocks falling from outer space, I think everyone will have to step up to the plate. That's all I'm trying to say."

The two Richards noticed in passing that some neighbor had covered Phil's body with an old tarp. Other than that, everyone was now hiding in their homes. The parents walked into the house and went to the kitchen James and Janice were taking perishables out of the refrigerator and into the two coolers. This included some ice packs and loose ice cubes to keep the items cold for at least some period.

"Good job, Janice and James. I'll get some boxes for some canned and dry goods."

"Why? Why not just run the storm generator for the refrigerator?" Jean asked.

"Because we need to leave the area. I told you—"

"And I told you, Jack, that I am not leaving just because there are some problems. If nothing else, they will need trained medical staff to help with all the casualties. To include for people who lose it and start shooting people."

An exasperated sigh, Jack replied. "See those columns of smoke? They are getting closer, which means the fires are spreading. With more fires when more meteors come down."

"Meteorites, Father. They hit the Earth." James said.

"Whatever you call them. Three in the last half hour have dome unimaginable damage."

"Where are the rest, Jack? There are no more, no matter the damage they caused. Meteors come in showers I bet you they are passed. So no need to leave now."

"Father, Mother, the President was on the radio," interjected James.

"What did he say?" Asked Jean.

"This is a natural disaster of biblical proportions, but the United States Government will help my fellow Americans to rebuild, and recover from their losses."

Jack and Jean knew that, based on James' thought processes and speaking pattern, he had spoken the President's exact words verbatim. Before the two parents could argue more, Jean called out.

"Mom, Dad. Look at this." Jean was at the back sliding door. As she spoke, there was a thump against the side of the house. Jack and Jean looked out through the reinforced glass of the sliding door.

"My God," exclaimed Jean.

Squirrels, cats, raccoons, even some rats were clambering over or squeezing under the back wooden fence. They were all fleeing something. When the wind blew some smoke and soot into the backyard, the Richards knew what that something was, it was burning houses.

"Come on, move," commanded Jack. "We leave in five minutes."

"But our home, our things…" said Jean.

"They can be replaced. We can't," answered Jack. "Come on. Grab some things you want to save and let's go."

"Okay." Jean's tone was of a person who had to accept the unacceptable, with no hope of change.

The four J's rushed around and packed the SUV as fast as they could. Jack had to open the garage door by hand there being no power. He helped his children stuff the food, coolers, sleeping bags, and the Bug Out bags into the back of the vehicle. Jean showed up with the EMT bag, some stuffed toys and a couple of photo albums.

"At least we'll have memories," Jean said. James jammed two bows and quivers of arrows in the back of the SUV. Jack smiled at his son.

"Smart, James. Those target bows will at least take down small game once we run out of store-bought food."

"Thanks, Father. I try to be smart."

"We're going to kill squirrels, maybe rabbits?" Janice asked with a frown.

"If we have to, honey," Jack answered.

"Are you going to keep Mike's pistol?" Jean asked

"I'm sure as hell not going to give it back to him and have a murder-suicide on my conscience."

"Language, Father... I forgot the Curse Jar." James started to open the SUV door.

"Forget it, James. We have more important things to worry about."

"My friends," said Janice in a low tone. "I can't get a call through on my cell phone to tell them where we are going."

"911 calls have the circuits jammed, dear. That will have to wait. Let's go." Jack backed the SUV out of the garage. As he did, some cinders flew past the windshield.

"James. Shut the garage door. Hurry, we have to move," directed Jack.

James jumped out, slammed the door shut, then jumped back in the vehicle.

"Hang on," said Jack.

The father accelerated down the hill towards the lower roads. He thanked his stars that he had filled up the oversized fuel tank of the late model SUV. Jack saw a hot red cinder fly by, sucked into the SUV's vortex as he accelerated away from the neighborhood. Jack did not look back.

Jack drove North as the morning sky was blackened by burning neighborhoods. The Richards had listened to the EBS on the car radio, there still being some stations on the air. The Government was again telling people to shelter in place, which slowed the initial panic flight outside the population centers. Another substantially sized rock hit Bangor Submarine Base on the Kitsap Penninsula. The third rock/meteor Jack had seen heading towards Joint Base Lewis/McChord had struck a fuel storage area which had added to the conflagrations in the area. It was the size of a basketball according to the news reports but hit with sufficient force to eject flaming debris out onto the Base offices and living areas. There were not enough firefighting units to fight all the fires, especially the now vast one on the hill areas in Puyallup. A basketball-sized meteor one had also hit in downtown Seattle. Everything was going to Hell in a handbasket.

Jack stayed off the Interstates and major highways. He took The East Valley Highway out of Puyallup then took state and county roads that ran parallel in a northerly direction. Sure enough, Military convoys and groups of First Responder vehicles soon tied up the highways and streets. Most businesses were shut after the Federal Government had given the Shelter in Place direction. Up around Duval. Jack saw an open Stop and Rob store with gas pumps that were open. He pulled in and up to the pumps.

"Okay, please listen up," Jack said. "I know we rushed out of our home, which may or may not be a pile of ashes but we could not take a chance of being trapped and burnt to death. And, we have the eight hundred pound gorilla in the room that we had some…nasty words exchanged yesterday." He looked at Jean and Janice, then continued.

"If the fact that we had one neighbor shoot another out of seemingly the clear blue sky, just remember that a worldwide threat of mass destruction seems to become fact, which will result in even more people losing it. So, we Four Js have to have each other's backs. Okay?"

There was silence other than the SUV engine noise. Then Janice spoke. "Look, I'm sorry I was so damned angry yesterday. Mom, James, I love you both. Sorry."

Jack knew that the apology Janice just gave was hard as she did not want to admit her feelings were not real or justified. Jack looked at Jean. She sighed, then spoke.

"I'm sorry I slapped you, Janice. And I'm sorry that your brother—" She glanced at James, pausing. "We love you dearly, James. Being different can cause problems when dealing with other people. They are not your fault. They just… happened." She looked her son.

"Well, Father, Mother, Sister," said James. "I wished I was normal all the time, but even so-called ordinary people are not always rational. Just look at our dead neighbor."

"Well put, Son, but you have nothing to apologize about," stated Jack.

"I don't want to be a burden, Father."

"You're not," said Jean as she reached over the seat and hugged her son. Janice and Jack reached over as best they could, and it turned into a group hug.

As they broke the clinch, Jack said, "Everyone check to see how much cash they have. I don't think anybody will be able to run credit cards."

"Damn," said Jean. "I was going to get some cash today. I only have a few ones."

"I have a twenty and a few coins. Jack?"

"Five dollars and thirty- nine cents for lunch."

"I have a hundred," Janice responded matter of fact.

"Well, how did you turn into Miss Moneybags?"Asked Jack.

"I've been saving it for the Prom. You'll have to pay me back." No one mentioned the chance of a High School Prom was probably zip.

"Well, Daughter, I'm using my twenty to top off the gas tank. If you want to check out the store and get some batteries, extra toilet paper and anything else you can think of, please be my guest."

Jean and Janice went into the stop and rob and saw a weathered old man behind the counter. He had a radio on and had a fuzzy television channel on a black and white set older than the Richards.

"You have power?" Janice asked.

"It's been flickering, but the local substation is still working. None of those rocks have hit here yet. But Puyallup is going up in smoke." When he saw the looks on the two women's faces, he quickly added, "Sorry if you are from there. But reports are sketchy, and I seem to be the only store open."

"Batteries," Jean said. "Do you have batteries?"

"Over on that rack there," the store owner answered.

"There are a few flashlights there also."

Jack entered and laid a twenty on the counter. "Surprised you did not make me pay first, Mister…"

"Just call me Pops. Everyone around here does. I've had this store for over twenty years, I can tell those who are honest."

"Okay, Pops. Have you seen much on that television of yours?"

"There are massive fires around Puyallup, Tacoma, and the military base down there. Downtown Seattle is a mess as the top was knocked off of the old Smith Tower. And that is just local news."

"How about around the nation?" asked Jean as she brought an armful of batteries up to the counter.

"Ma'am, around the nation, around the world it's the same," replied Pops. "How in the Hell all those scientists and big government wigs missed the fact that asteroid had some tag-a-longs in the way of meteors I'll never know. But it has screwed everything up. People are dying and cities are burning all over."

Janice brought up some rolls of toilet paper to the registered, shook as she set them down. The wizened old man known as Pops looked at her, then spoke.

"Sorry if I upset you, young lady. But, well, you younger generation need to know what's happening so you can help us old farts to fix this. We are not doing a very good job right now."

"How much?" asked Jack.

"Give me another twenty, and we'll call it even. I can't very well charge tax when there is no one to collect it. As the fires spread, a few more rocks hit, there won't be anybody worrying about things like sales tax."

"Thanks, Sir. By the way, you wouldn't have any shotgun ammo, would you?"

"Not for sale," Pops answered. "Not licensed for it, but here." Pops reached under the counter and came up with a beat up five round box. "I have a twelve gauge behind the counter here. This old box has three buckshot and two slug rounds."

"Thanks, Pops. Anything we can do for you?" Asked Jack.

"Yeah. Be careful. I was a Marine in Saigon when South Viet Nam collapsed, and we tried to evacuate people at the last minute." Pops looked at the mother and daughter. "People do really nasty things when they panic. Even the best of them."

"Thanks again," said Jean.

"No problem. Hope to see you again."

James was waiting by the SUV. He was looking back South. "Father, the sky is getting blacker, smokier," stated James.

"Yes, James. It will get darker as the fires spread." Jack motioned to the two women. "Hop in. Time to thread our way North." After all four family members were belted in, Jack paused with his hand on the ignition key. "What Pops said about people panicking, then being nasty, take that to heart." He turned his head and looked at his family. "We have each other. If something bad happens, if we become separated, you need to help whomever you are with. This really applies to you, James and Janice."

"Dad," Janice started to interject, but Jack stopped her.

"Look, I mean it. No matter what happens, you two need to look out for each other, take care of each other, no matter how pissed off you are."

"Language, Father," James said.

"Forget that right now, James. Listen to what I just said. You are both going to have to step up to the plate, Okay? No matter what problems you have."

The Richards sat silent for a minute. Then Jack turned the ignition key, and the SUV roared into life.

"I filled the gas tank up to the brim, so no matter how many detours we make, we should have enough gas to get to Uncle Mark's cabin."

"Father," said James.

"Yes, Son."

"I'm hungry."

"Here," Jean said as she produced a plastic storage bag from her large purse. "I saved the bacon from the breakfast I tried to make. Who wants some?"

Everyone said 'me' at once, and the tension broke as they began to laugh.

4

Typically, a trip to the cabin near Buck Creek in the Snoqualmie National Forest area would have taken half a day. This day, September 13th, it took some twelve hours. Jack stayed to State Roads and anything that ran parallel to Interstate Five until he hit State Road 530 which ran approximately West to East from the Arlington area to Darrington, Washington. Whenever he was near a freeway or a significant highway, Jack saw emergency vehicles running hither and yon at high speeds. Jack and the family also saw bizarre sights of burning cars in clumps, sometimes with no first responders around. What was going on?

The Four J's were finally on State Road 530 headed East towards Darrington. It was not a large town just a few thousand people in and around the Darrington area. State Road 530 headed northeast from Darrington, up towards the roads in and around the Buck Creek Area where the cabin was located. There was also a Sauk-Suiatte Tribal area and reservation, to include a small casino. As Jack drove the SUV from the main Darrington area. He looked around. It seemed like most people were following the "shelter in place" instructions until the Government was sure the meteor shower was over. A couple of commercial radio stations were still broadcasting EBS information. Thus the Richards family heard about a couple more rocks which had struck around the Seattle/Tacoma area causing more devastation. Lewis-McChord was no longer an operational military base after a rock the size of an old Volkswagen car had slammed into the middle of the airfield at such an angle that a basketball-sized chunk broke off and zipped up and over, coming down near American Lake and the Veterans Administration center. Another rapidly growing fire spread, engulfing suburbia around the military installation. Casualties were estimated to be at least in the thousands.

During these broadcasts, a new threat was mentioned. Apparently small groups of what could only be described as Feral human beings were preying on anybody on the road. Law Enforcement was trying to get a handle on these miscreants, but with all the destructive fires and the damage caused by the bomb like impacts of the meteorites, organized government control was hit and miss. As the Richards left Darrington on them journey northeast, they saw a couple of cars in the ditches along the road, one on each side of State Road 530.   As Jack slowed, a man stepped out from a small clump of brush. The man was bearded and scruffy, his greasy brown hair hanging in tangle threads. The bearded man waved them down, as Jack saw another man coming from the car in the ditch on the other side of the road. Jack rolled down the window.

"What happened?" Jack asked.

"A wreck, of course," the scruffy man said with an unfriendly grin. "Where ya going?"

"Up the road," said Jack, motioning with his chin.

"Family, huh," said Mister Scruffy. "Lots of food?"

"Jack," Jean said with a worried tone. Jack chanced a glance at the man coming from the wrecked car. The late summer sunlight enabled Jack to see the man had blood on his hands and shirt. It did not look like his.

"Got any booze?" asked Mister Scruffy. The man started to reach under his shirt. Jack had the pistol he had taken from Mike pointed in Mister Scruffy's face before he finished his action.

"Move back, and don't pull out whatever in under your shirt until we are gone." The man's eyes were a bit wide as he stepped back and slowly raised his hands. The man approaching from the wreck stepped in front of the SUV. When he saw his comrade raise his hands, he started to reach for the small of his back. Jack stomped on the accelerator, and the sizeable V-8 engine under the hood of the SUV responded. The partner of Mister Scruffy tried to pull a pistol from under his shirt at the same time he attempted to jump from the path of the large vehicle. The man succeeded in neither action. The right fender struck him as Janice screamed. The attacker was spun towards the wrecked car he had just departed, the pistol knocked flying from his grasp.

"Down!" Jack yelled as steered the SUV to the center of the road. A gunshot echoed from behind the family, and there was a twanging thump as something struck the tailgate. Jack swerved the SUV right, then left. Another shot rang out, and the back driver's side window cracked from the impact of the bullet, but the safety glass held together. Jack swerved a bit then accelerated straight ahead. There were no more gunshots.

Jack kept hauling ass until Jean said," Honey, we are coming up on the casino." With that, he took his foot off the gas pedal and let the SUV coast. He drove the car into the casino parking lot and braked. He placed the gearshift into park, and leaned back, shaking.

"Everyone okay?" he asked. "Anybody hit?"

"No, Father," replied James as if being shot at happened every day. "The window is broken."

"Dad, why-why did they do that, shoot at us?" Janice

asked, her chin quivering.

"Because they are scum, Janice," answered Jean.

"Father, a policeman is coming." At James' statement, Jack looked up. A car marked Tribal Police pulled up in front of the SUV. Jack turned the engine off as he stuck the pistol under his left thigh, hoped it could not be seen. The police officer, a young Sauk-Suiatte male, frowned at the window with the bullet hole.

"Trouble?" the officer asked.

"Yes," answered Jean. "Some assholes tried to rob us. My husband had to run one over."

The young man grunted acknowledgment. "Why didn't you shelter in place as the President said?"

"Officer, we're supposed to meet my Brother, Mark Richards up here. We were traveling when..."

"Mark Richards? You must be Jack," the young man said, his mouth forming a grin.

"You know Mark?" Jean asked.

"Yes, Ma'am. He hangs around the casino, helped with a few government matters when the Tribe was having an argument with some bureaucrats. Your Mark seems to have some interesting contacts."

Jack chuckled as he answered. "Yes, he always had a bit of 'maverick' in him, seemed to foster unique connections and friendships."

"I'm Officer Forest," stated the patrolman. "So you were shaken down by some people down the road?"

"They tried, but we got away."

"Father..." James started to say something and Janice poked him in the ribs said 'shhh' under his breath.

"I'll drive down and see if they are still hanging around," the patrolman said.

"There were two cars in the ditch. I don't know who caused it, but one guy had some blood on his clothes that did not look like his."

"Thanks. I'll be careful. Your brother's cabin should be okay. I check it because it's on the edge of the tribal land, he's a friend, so..." He trailed off.

"Thank You, officer. Be careful. Everything is nuts," added Jack.

Officer Forest moved his vehicle, and Jack drove the SUV from the parking lot.

"Whew. That was close," said Jack. "I'm still glad I have Mike's pistol."

"I wish it weren't necessary," stated Jean. "I don't like guns."

"But Father saved us," James said from the back seat. "And the pistol helped."

"Yes it did, James," answered Jack. "But hopefully we don't have to depend on it."

"But what if we did, Father? What if things get worse, more meteorites hit?"

Jack sighed. Oft times he and Jean forgot just how sharp their son was under all the fog of his condition. Thus, he often asked hard questions.

"Well, Son, one thing at a time. We need to get to the cabin first." Jack glanced in the rearview mirror. "Janice? You okay?"

Janice shifted in the SUV backseat.

"I'm just scared, Dad. I miss our house already."

"We're all scared, Janice. But we have each other," interjected her Mother.

Janice undid her seatbelt leaned up and hugged her mother, then her father. "I do love you, even if I get nasty sometimes," she said. James leaned over and tried to hug them all. "Group hug!" he stated as he tried to wrap his arms around them all.

"Hey, Bud. Wait until the cabin. I'm driving here," said Jack.

"Okay, Father. Seat belts back on."

The family reached the cabin off a dirt road that ran near Buck Creek. The area was a small section that Uncle Mark had somehow arranged to be ceded to him, with the help of the Tribal Government. There, he had constructed a Loft Cabin for all family members to enjoy. Mark was still single, probably Jack surmised due to his employment and lifestyle. All Jack thought of now was that he was glad they had this safe haven of escape.

"Alright, James and Janice. Start unloading stuff. I'll get the front door," Jack directed. The front door was a unique combination lock connected to an alarm system. The windows and back door all had bars over them with quick release mechanisms in case of fire. Jack punched in the combination to the front door, and it unlocked. He went in and towards a small access stairway which led to a combination root cellar and bomb shelter. Down in the cellar was a storage battery system connected to a solar panel powered system that kept a trickle charge going into the batteries when the cabin was unoccupied. A few switches and viola, electric power and lights.

Jack went back up the stairs to meet Jean supervising the offloading of the SUV. She had opened the back door to get some fresh air circulating, there was the typical musty smell of rooms closed up for an extended time. She smiled, then grabbed Jack and kissed him.

"Thanks for keeping us safe, Aero Man."

"Anytime, Tooth Fairy."

"Father, where do you want the bow and arrows?" interrupted Jack.

"Keep them near at hand, James. I'll get the shotgun from the car." James walked back to the SUV.

"Does Mark keep any weapons here?"

"He has a high powered crossbow in the cellar, that's it."

"Just want to make sure there are not any loaded weapons someone could accidentally... set off."

Jack knew arguing with Jean over this subject would do no good. She still had this fear that James, because of his 'condition,' would get a hold of a weapon and hurt himself or others. He saw now was not the time to try and disburse her of that fear.

"I'll keep everything under control, okay Tooth Fairy?"

Jean smiled as she answered. "Okay, Aero Man."

A half hour and everything from the SUV was stashed away in various cupboards and storage areas. Mark had a half-sized refrigerator he obtained from some out of business motel hooked to the solar power system. The Four Js jammed as many perishables from the coolers as they could.

As they looked at what would not fit, Jean said, "I feel an ice cream craving coming on." She grinned at her two children. "Want to join me?"

Jack laughed and joined in. They sat around the kitchen table that doubled as a dining table and shared two gallons of ice cream, one chocolate, one vanilla-raspberry swirl. As they ate, they talked without the distraction of cell phones, television, and computers.

"What do you think, Dad? When will this all blow over?" asked Janice. Jack shrugged.

"It may take a while for the federal and state governments to get enough cops and the military out and about to take care of people like those assholes as well as help those people injured and displaced. We are lucky you have an Uncle who planned ahead for just such a disaster."

"You think it's a natural disaster of biblical proportions like the President said?" his wife asked.

"What else could it be? I don't see the Russians or Chinese going to all the trouble of dropping rocks on their own heads to get back at us."

"Aliens." It took a moment to realize James had spoken.

"What do you mean, Son?" Asked Jack.

"The rocks might have been launched from asteroid 18666. Lots of authors like Heinlein, Asimov, Arthur C. Clark.

Larry Niven, Bear, Brin, wrote about how alien species could bombard their enemies with pieces of asteroids, broken satellites, all types of space junk. Enough would get through without burning up to act like artillery strikes. Just like shells people used in World War Two, Desert Storm, and the Iraq War."

Everyone sat quietly for a moment. Then Janice spoke. "Why? Why would some…things come millions of miles for a rock fight?"

James shrugged. "Because they are Aliens. They don't think like you."

"But they may think like you?" Janice replied.

"Maybe," James said. Jean started to interrupt and defuse a possible argument, but James beat her to the punch. "I know I'm different. I know sometimes my brain does weird things. At least everyone around me thinks it's weird." James paused for a moment, then continued. "But who's to say how I think sometimes, and act sometimes is not standard to some alien race."

"A race of James'?" Janice said.

"Why not? I'm good looking, smart. I just act a little off sometimes."

Jack thought for a second that James was trying to be funny. Then he realized he was being serious. James' was demonstrating a level of introspection that completely surprised them all.

"You know we love you, James," said his Mother.

"And I love you all," James replied. "But I am different. So you may love an alien."

"Well, Son, you have not turned green yet, so I don't think you're from Venus."

James laughed, something he rarely did since reaching his 'teens.' Jack always worried he was not happy because he didn't laugh much anymore.

"But if I turned green, would you still love me, Father,

Mother?"

Jean teared up. She pushed back her chair, reached over and hugged her son. "James, I carried you in my body for nine months to the day. I don't do that for just anyone." She kissed his forehead. James hugged her back, then Janice slid over and joined in.

"Group hug," Jack said and joined in. The stayed in the group clinch for a minute, then separated.

"Come on, Janice," Jean said. "Help your old mom make up the beds in the loft. I for one am worn out."

"Okay, Mom." The two womenfolk climbed the winding staircase to the loft and left the two menfolk downstairs.

"Come here, James, let me show you something." Jack walked over at recovered the shotgun from near the front door.

"Remember this? That time we went out with Uncle Mark?"

"Yes, Father. And I shot several guns but we did not tell Mother." Jack laughed.

"Yeah, please don't mention it. I don't think she would be happy about that. Anyway, here is the loading gate for the shells, you work the slide to jack a round into the chamber. Safety is here. I just put a slug round in it from that box Pops gave us. Don't shot anything you don't expect to destroy."

"Yes, Father." James took the shotgun from Jack, raised it to his shoulder and sighted down the barrel as if he did it every day.

"You remember everything from that day, don't you James?"

"Yes, Father. I remember everything when I am having fun. I disremember things that were not fun."

Jack looked intently at his Son. He knew at that moment that James would be alright no matter what happened. Someday James would be on his own. But he would handle it.

"James, why do you call me Father instead of Dad like a lot of your peers do their fathers."

James looked him straight in the eyes.

"Because I love and respect you, Father. You are better than a Dad."

Jack tried not to tear up, but he did anyway.

"Father, it is okay to cry. It is normal for men to cry. I do."

Jack hugged his Son. He knew he could never ask for a better child.

It was 7:00 PM, Pacific Standard Time. Jean and Janice were up in the loft making up the two beds. The family would have to share the beds, although there was a giant stuffed sofa downstairs.

"There, honey. That should do it." Jean smiled at her daughter.

"Mom." Janice looked down. "I'm really sorry I said all those things... about you and James."

"Come here," Jean said. Then she hugged her daughter. "All those things you said... there is not a week that goes by that I don't wonder if what I did during my wild days caused James' condition. Then I had this perfect baby girl, and I thought maybe God had played a cruel joke on me." She stepped back from Janice and held her hands.

"I rebelled against my dad and mom, as there were strict. My Dad was a cop, so he expected me to stay out of trouble, not run around with the rough kids. My mom had a tendency to thump the Bible too much. So, I rebelled."

Jean sniffed.

"So I tried things I shouldn't have, slept around, was in the back of a police car a couple of times."

"Then you met Dad?" Janice asked.

"Yep. Jack was a college senior, had talked to the U.S. Air Force about Officers Training School after he had his Aerospace Engineering Degree. I was taking classes part-time, working at dead-end jobs, just screwing around with no focus." Jean laughed. "He had enough focus for both of us. But he was so damned nice! Never pushed me to do anything. But I realized I wanted to do things to make him happy, wanted him to respect me. Because I loved him." Jean paused for a moment. "He told me he loved me and that was it. We waited until he was Commissioned and had been on the job a year before we were married. I crammed as much school into that year as I could."

"Then you joined him?" asked Janice.

"Yep. I studied my butt off for the next three years. Wound up aiming for dental surgery, Jack saw an aerospace career outside of the Air Force, as he never had the 'eyes' to be a Pilot. In the Air Force, if you aren't a pilot, you are a second-class citizen. So, he went into the Reserves and never looked back. I got my medical degree, started working in a clinic. Then we had James." Jean took a deep breath, then let it out.

She looked into Janice's eyes. "I need to ask you a big favor."

"What, Mom?"

"Promise you and James will always take care of each other? I know he can be difficult, but he loves you, would do anything for you."

"Mom, I love him. I just get frustrated. You were young. In high school, girls want to have fun, meet and date great looking boys." Janice paused for a moment in thought.

"But after today, I see how easy everything can fall apart. So, Yes, Mom. I promise we will take care of each other, no matter what. But you aren't going anywhere. So you get to help."

Mother and Daughter embraced, then parted.

"Let's let your Dad and Brother know the beds are made, and I for one am going to crash."

"I think, Mom, that is a great idea."

The Four J's met in the small living room and discussed their plans.

"You ladies and James can go to bed. I'm going to stay up until it's dark. Then. I think I'll sleep down here on the sofa."

Jean frowned as she spoke. "Still worried someone may show up?"

"Maybe. Also that the meteor shower isn't over. So, I'll stay up."

"Can I stay up with you, Father?" asked James. His Father looked at him, then answered.

"Okay, young man. If you want. Ladies, sleep tight, don't let the bed bugs bite."

"'Nite Dad, 'Nite James." Janice gave both of them a peck of a kiss.

"Come here, you," ordered Jean as she grabbed Jack in an embrace and gave him a long kiss.

"Jean, the kids—"

"—know about the birds and the bees... so don't worry."

Jack noticed his wife seemed to sway her nice hips a bit as she made her way up the small staircase. Maybe later, Jack thought, there would be a chance at 'alone time.'

"James, turn the radio on low, see if you can get an EBS report."

"Yes, Father."

It was 7:20 PM, Pacific Standard Time.

"...reports of strange sounds and lights, then of unusual aircraft are coming from various cities and states. The Federal Government is trying to verify that similar reports are coming from Russian and European sources. Meteors have devastated much of the worldwide communication systems even though there are reports that most near orbit satellites have been spared. Military sources are working to restore communication to…"

The cabin began to shake as a loud roaring engine noise seemed to appear from nowhere. Jack heard Janice let out a squeal up in the loft as bright lights shown through the cabin windows.

"What the…" Jack said as he looked at his son.

"They're here," James replied.

Whatever it was that passed overhead was more extensive than any military craft they had experienced living near an active duty base. Jack was frozen in place, unsure if he really wanted to go outside and look up at the machine passing over the cabin. When James started to move to the front door, Jack grabbed his arm.

"Don't. They may not have seen us." Jean and Janice managed to stumble down the vibrating stairs as the sky object finally seemed to pass by.

"What the hell was that?" Jean demanded.

"Aliens. They're here," answered James.

"James, we don't know that," Jack said.

"Yes, we do, Father. There is no aircraft that size around here. Not even a Boeing 747."

Jack knew that, but he thought if he didn't admit to it, it would not become a reality and scare Jean, Janice… and himself.

"Whatever it was, its headed south," Jack said. "Turn off all the lights, pull the drapes and curtains, stay down in the living room together. Safety in numbers."

"And you have a gun," Janice said. Even as she said it, Jack knew that it felt like a popgun in his hands when compared to the gigantic beast of an aircraft that had just passed.

"Yes, we have weapons, Janice. But its better if we stay

hidden."

"Your dad is right," Jean stated in support. "Let's get down by the sofa and stay quiet."

"I'll turn the radio off, Mother," James said. "We know as much as the radio people do now."

"Probably more, Son," added Jack.

The Four Js soon hunkered down by the sofa, wrapped up with a couple of blankets. They said little, just listened for the return of the unknown flying object. A half hour later, and Jack got to his feet and went to the front door.

"Honey," Jean said.

"Don't worry. I'm just going to take a peek." Jack slowly opened the door and stepped out onto the porch.

"Damn," he said, then stepped back into the cabin and bolted the door.

"What happened?" His wife asked.

"There is a large glow of lights from around where the Tribal Casino sits. It looks almost like someone set up a considerable carnival with rides and all."

"What are we going to do, Father?" Asked James.

"Stay low and out of sight and hope this all blows over." Jack looked at his two children. "Remember what your Mother and I have said. You two take care of each other if we get separated."

"Dad, you're scaring me," said Janice with a shiver.

"Isn't your brother Mark coming here?" asked Jean as she put her arm around her daughter.

"I have no idea. Damn. I just remembered. There is a small portable CB radio in the cellar. I might be able to hit somebody up that way."

"I tried the Internet on my notebook, Father. I could usually get a wifi signal from the casino. Nothing right now."

"Well, James, a lot of towers and lines are probably down. Hold the fort down while I use a flashlight to find that CB radio." Jack began to walk to the cellar stairs.

A human scream echoed outside. The Richards froze.

"Jack…"

"Stay down. I'll peek outside."

"Don't open the door, Dad," Janice said.

"I'll just peek outside…"

The human scream was closer to the cabin. With the second scream, Jack stepped to the door with the shotgun held at port arms, reverting back to his limited military training. He looked out the window next to the front door. There was enough ambient light from a clear sky and the light show from the area of the Sauk-Suiatt Indian Casino to illuminate a running figure. Despite all the cabin lights being off, the person ran straight to the cabin's front porch.

"Shit," Jack said under his breath as he realized the individual resembled Mister Scruffy from earlier in the day. The man screamed again, then fell as he tried to mount the few front steps to the porch.

"What's happening?" Jean called out.

"Stay back," directed Jack as he set the shotgun aside and unbolted the front door. He picked the twelve gauge back up, then opened the door. Mister Scruffy was lying face down on the porch, sobbing. His shirt was ripped, and there was a large bloody gash running across the man's back. Before Jack could say anything, Mister Scruffy jerked his head up and stared at Jack with wild eyes.

"They're after me! Hide me, please."

"Who is after you?" Demanded Jack.

"*Them*. Those things. They have wheels…" Mister Scruffy choked, coughed, then spewed blood all over the porch.

"Jean. I need your help."

His wife was up in a flash and near his side. She knelt down next to Mister Scruffy. "That gash on his back. He's spitting blood. He may have internal injuries from a fall, or something fell on him."

"Car wreck?" Jack asked.

"Maybe... Sir? I'm a doctor. I'm going to give you a quick examination..."

"*Them! Run!*" The wounded man jerked part way up off the porch, screamed, and then collapsed. Jean immediately tried to clear Mister Scruffy's airway, then stopped. She felt the side of his neck for a pulse. Jean stood up shaking her head.

"Dead. Maybe heart failure or internal injuries. Someone will have to cut the man open to find out." She began to shake a bit. Jack put his arm around her.

"I'll have James help me move the body."

"You think that's wise, Jack? You know..."

"I know everyone is going to have to step up, as of now. Trust me. He'll rise to the..." Jack stopped talking. He cocked his head.

"Jean, you hear a whirring noise, like a large electric motor?"

"I think so, Jack..."

A large and extremely bright floodlight lit up the front porch and the dead body. Jack and Jean cried out in surprise as they tried to cover their eyes, saw spots from the brightness of the light. Jack managed to shove Jean back through the open door and shut it by feel. Janice screamed, and James called out as he moved toward the door. "Father! Mother!"

"James. Watch your eyes. Something with an extremely bright light is outside. See if you can see what's happening." Jack tried to shake and rubbed the spots in front of his eyes away as Jean stumbled to the couch and Janice. James put his hands over his eyes, then cracked his fingers minutely. There was a scraping sound from the front porch, then the sound of a loud electric motor, whirring.

"Father," James said in a hushed voice, "there is an oversized ATV out in the driveway by the SUV. It has an oversized beach ball-shaped turret or dome emanating from the vehicle body. It looks like the source of the floodlight. And, a metal tentacle just dragged the man's body to it."

James could be very observant and precise when he was in the right frame of mind. Tonight, he was just that.

Jack's eyes were finally clear enough that he could see between the spots and splotches.

"Get back, James, before it sees you." James stepped back, then turned and sat on the edge of the couch.

"It's a robot, Father."

"How can you tell, Son.?

"It moves like one. Single-minded it was chasing the man, found him. Mission accomplished."

"We need to leave, Jack," interjected Jean.

"How, Honey? If we try to drive off in the SUV, the friends of that... 'robot' will notice."

"There's more?" Janice asked.

"Yes," said James. "That oversized craft is big enough to carry hundreds, maybe even thousands."

"Now, Son," said Jack. "Let's not jump to conclusions on numbers. But someone or something is behind the robot, directing it." He looked at his family, tried to formulate a plan of survival. "James, Janice, grab your Bug Out Bags, a couple of blankets. Jean, grab some cans of food, water, some matches I saw by the wood stove. We'll sneak out back, and hide in the woods."

"Why not stay here?" Jean asked.

"Because that wheeled robot at least noticed us. It will be back when it gets new orders."

"We could hide in the cellar," said Janice.

"Then we would have no back door. We'd be trapped. Come on. Get the stuff for a night in the woods. By then maybe those things will be—"

Something long, metal and sharp smashed thru the drape covered front window. It missed Janice by inches as her mother screamed.

"James, take Janice out the back, *now!*" Jack saw the

spear-like object was more like a harpoon with a thin metallic line attached. He scrambled to the broken front window as the wheeled robot near the front porch tried to pull the harpoon loose and back for another shot. He pushed the drapes back enough for a quick sight picture and let rip with the shotgun. As Jack fired, Janice felt surprisingly strong arms grab her, lift her up and carry her towards the back door.

"Jack, Pistol!" Jean yelled.

"Kitchen table," he called back as he racked a new shell into the shotgun chamber and fired. A crackling sound and a smell of ozone and burning wiring came from in front of the cabin. Then Jean was next to him with the pistol.

"You hate guns," Jack said.

"My Dad taught me how to shoot, he was a cop, remember?" Jean answered. A harpoon smashed through the cabin front door, then was reeled back by another wheeled robot, taking the door with it.

"Shit!" Jack exclaimed. "Out the back, Jean." The two adults raced towards the back exit. A six-wheeled oversized ATV like robot slammed through the front doorway. Jack swung around and fired at the new threat just as a metal tentacle snaked out and grabbed his left leg. He was yanked off his feet. Jean screamed, turned and emptied the nine-millimeter pistol into the beach ball shaped turret just as it's floodlight started to flash. Sparks flew from the now destroyed light, then the robot began to spark and short out like a cheap toaster. Jean dropped the empty pistol, reached down and tried to pull Jack up. But the metal tentacle would not let go. Jean screamed with rage, grabbed a standing metal living room lamp with a weighted bottom and began to smash it into the metal tentacle. Two good whacks and it released its grasp.

Jack lurched to his feet, began reaching into a pocket for more shotgun shells.

Jean started pulling him toward the back door.

"Come on! The pistols empty and the kids are running."

"Okay. Love you, Tooth Fairy."

"Love you too, Aero—" A harpoon smashed through a side window.

Janice had not realized James was this strong until her brother picked her up and sprinted out the back door. She had a hold of a blanket and James seemed to have something across his back. Neither fact seemed to slow him down. James ran up a trail that led to a small lookout point on a mountain foothill. Janice always had liked that spot, watched the sunset as the colors reflected off the forest and the Cascades. Now it was a place of safety, not beauty.

James ran for a good five minutes flat out. How he did that carrying her, Janice would never know. But his speed ate up the distance to the lookout even when he began to slow. Then they were there, at the lookout. James slowed, carried her to a small stone bench someone had constructed, set her down, and then collapsed.

"James! Are you alright? Answer me! If you just killed yourself, I'll…"

"I… am… okay," he managed to choke out between gasps for air. Janice hugged her brother, let go when he started coughing.

"Need… air… please… Sister."

"How in the hell did you do that, James? Carry me like that."

"Language, Sister," James replied.

"Answer me. How?"

"Because I had to… Father told me to take you to safety. So I did."

Janice knew that once her brother became single-minded about doing something, almost fixated, he got things done. Sometimes people did not understand why he wanted to do things, but when he did, he always finished. Like when he took the clothes dryer apart. However, in this case, it saved her.

"Thanks, James." Janice paused. "Mom, Dad. They're not

following us. We have to go back."

"No, Sister. We cannot."

"Why not?" Janice began to become angry. "Look, we left them there. *You* left them there. We have to—"

"Don't you see? Why can't you, Janice?" James' face began to flush. "Those robots have Mother and Father. They sacrificed for us. For *us*! That is why I was told to take you. Don't you see?" Tears began to run down his face. James rarely cried or let on he was hurt. He had reached a breaking point Janice had never seen before.

Janice grabbed and hugged her brother.

"I'm sorry all the nasty things I said about you," she said as she began to cry. All the fear and realization of what had happened washed over her in a wave.

"Mom and Dad. *Gone*," Janice said between sobs.

"We have each other, Sister. We need to take care of each other as they said."

The two siblings stayed clinched in their grief for a minute, then separated. "Now what?" asked Janice as she wiped her eyes with her shirt sleeve.

"I think we stay here. I grabbed my bugout bag, and you have a blanket. We stay here until daylight, sneak on back down to the cabin and see what we can salvage."

"I see you also grabbed a bow and a quiver of arrows."

"Father said to keep them at hand. So I did." Janice looked around at the peaceful clearing. Some of the ambient light from the Tribal Casino area ate at the darkness but did not destroy the natural ambiance.

"Mom always said the tall Douglas Firs gave this place the look of a cathedral, a natural church."

"This is a good place, Sister. We can rest and hide. I'll make a fire in the morning when it is safer."

"Well, James, let's find a few pine boughs and make a bed, as they showed us in Scouts."

Keeping busy helped dull the pain of loss. The two young adults made bedding of fir tree boughs, then cuddled as close as they could for warmth and pulled the blanket around themselves. They were on the edge of the clearing and in the shadows, so if anything came up the trail hopefully, they would not be seen.

"Good night, James," Janice mumbled. Then she fell into the sleep of exhaustion. James stayed awake for a few minutes and listened to his sisters even breathing.

"What would Father do?" he whispered to himself. Then he drifted off into sleep.

Morning sunlight through the trees and a cawing crow woke them. Since it was still Summer, the night had not been cold. But they were still a bit stiff from the unusual sleeping arrangements. James gave his sister a roll of toilet paper from his Bug Out Bag pack. He took the bow and arrows, then walked part way down the path he had run up. James stopped, listened, and looked. There was no sign anything or anyone had followed them up the trail. He turned and walked back to the clearing. Janice was rolling up the blanket and used a length of a vine to tie it up tight. As James stepped up, she tossed him back the roll of Toilet Paper.

"Thanks, Brother. Now what?"

"I went part way down the trail. There are no signs of anybody but us coming up here. I say we sneak down and check out the cabin."

"Sounds good. Do you have water?"

"Here. Just this one bottle."

Janice sipped and handed it back. James took a sip, then

put it in his pack. Without further conversation, they began slowly walking down the trail.

The stopped every minute or so, looked and listened. No more electric motors or flashing floodlights were seen or heard. They paused when the cabin came in sight.

"See anything, James?"

"No. Look, the back door is still open."

"Should we go in?"

"Yes." James fit an arrow on the bowstring. The two siblings began a slow walk to the back door. Other than an occasional bird call, there was no noise. The tiptoed up the small back porch and into the cabin. There was no sign of anyone.

They walked into the living room and saw the damage the harpoon objects had done to Uncle Mark's cabin. Any moment, Janice thought she would find a vast pool of blood, but there wasn't any.

She whispered to James. "No blood. They—those robots—may have taken Mom and Dad alive."

"We can hope, Sister. We can hope." Janice found her small pack and recovered two of the sleeping bags. James saw the pistol but not the shotgun. He put the empty semi-auto in his backpack with the hope of finding ammunition later on. James then went into the kitchen and loaded his backpack up with water bottles. Janice joined him in the kitchen, threw a couple cans of soda in her pack and then went to the refrigerator. It was still relatively cold, so she grabbed the condiments, lunchmeat, and cheese. Janice found a loaf of bread and threw some sandwiches together. She stuffed the last few unused slices of bread in her pack along with some bologna and cookies. Next, Janice split the sandwiches up with James. She looked at her brother.

"What's next, James?"

"Stay away from the roads. I think if we follow Buck Creek we wind up down by Wenatchee. At least I remember a trail on a map that seemed to show that. Buck Creek Trail."

Janice shrugged as she answered. "Sounds good to me. The SUV is out front. I guess that would be like sugar is to ants when it comes to the robots." She snapped her fingers. "Moms, EMT bag. It's not small, but we can carry it between us." Janice bounded up the stairs, James heard her rummaging in the loft.

"Got it! Let's go, James."

As Janice scrambled down the loft stairs with the sturdy bag, she saw James standing like a statue. He held up a finger as if for silence, then pointed toward the front porch. Through the broken front door, the sound of an approaching electric motor vehicle could be heard.

"The back door," whispered Janice. James grabbed the end strap of the large EMT bag as Janice grabbed the front one. Out the back, they hurried, and then towards the trail to the lookout point. As they rushed to from whence they had just come, Janice began to whisper a refrain to herself.

"Move along, nothing to see here, move along Alien Robot, nothing to see here."

The two siblings had just begun to disappear among the Douglas Firs which bracketed the trail when a bright light flashed off to their right. A patch of dry grass burst into flames.

"*Run!*" James yelled out. The whirring of the oversized electric motor of the robot was drawing nearer. James dropped his end of the EMT bag and yelled, "*Run!*" again. He turned around and notched an arrow on the bowstring. No sooner had James turned than a metal tentacle flew out and wrapped around his left leg. He yelled as he was yanked off his feet. Janice turned to look and screamed. She dropped the EMT bag, bent over and grabbed a good size rock from the edge of the trail, then ran screaming like a banshee at the alien robot.

"Let go of him, you damned dirty alien piece of shit!"

Just as Janice threw her missile, there was a loud report from off to her right. A substantially sized hole appeared in the side of the robot's turret dome. Another 'boom' followed, and another hole was punched in the dome, followed in quick succession by a third. The oversized beach ball shaped turret began to spit sparks from the bullet holes, then to spin around, faster and faster as more flashes appeared. Smoke billowed from the machine, and it ground to a halt. James kicked at the tentacle holding onto him, and it went limp. He rose to his feet, shaking. Both he and Janice looked at a figure advancing from out of the trees.

"We need to get out of here," the male called out.

"We're going up this trail," James answered.

"Sounds good," the figure answered. "Let's go."

James and Janice quickly retrieved the EMT kitbag and hustled up the trail to the lookout spot. The unknown male followed some hundred yards behind. The siblings were soon sitting on the stone bench as they watched the person approach.

"Friend?" Janice whispered to James.

"I guess. The guy shot the robot." James stood up as the male approached. He put his hand out to shake as his Father had taught him.

"James Richards. This is my Sister Janice. Thanks for saving us."

The person was a tall young man, close to James and Janice's age. He had the slightly darker skin of the local Native American peoples. His long black hair was tied back. He took James' hand and shook it.

"No problem. Is that your cabin I passed? "

"Our Uncle Mark's," answered Janice. That produced a small smile on the young man's face.

"My Uncle Buck and my Father know him and says he is quite the character. My name is Matt Bearclaw. Salish Puyallup." Matt looked around. "I think we need to head south. Those wheeled robots are all over."

"You live around here?" asked Janice.

"No, I live near Puyallup. I come up here to hunt black

bear and coyote with my .44 Magnum Marlin. Tribal affiliation so I hunt all over on traditional lands. Now, can we move? And what's in that big bag?"

"EMT Kit. It was my mom's," Janice said. She teared up a bit as she mentioned her mother. Matt looked at her, then reached his hand out.

"I can help carry. All I have is my rifle. My camp by the Buck Creek Campsite is crawling with those damned six-wheeled assholes."

"We have some food, this bow," James stated.

"Match made in Heaven, as my Mother used to say."

"You know Buck Creek Trail?" asked James.

"Yep," Replied Matt. " Hiked it many a time while looking for game. That'll do if we are going southbound. Then what?"

James and Janice looked at each other, shrugged in unison.

"Well, Puyallup is trashed," said Matt.

"Yeah, we just beat the meteors and fires as we left for here," replied Janice.

"So I guess when we reach the Leavenworth and Wenatchee area, we make a decision then, okay?" asked Matt.

"Yes, that sounds good." Said, James.

The next hour, Matt led them through the woods north of Darrington. The Tribal member took them wide around the Buck Creek Camp Ground he had fled.

"You don't think the robots may have left?" James asked

"I don't want to chance it. I'll just have to ask you to share your food with me until I have a chance to hunt."

As they walked, unfamiliar delta-shaped aircraft swooped low at sound barrier-busting speeds. The low-level shockwaves shook the forest, upsetting all the local fauna. Animals of all types were on the move.

"Well, we'll have fresh meat when we need it," said Matt.

"Do you know where your family is?" Janice asked.

"Nope. My Dad and Uncle were supposed to meet me at the campsite. Then the aliens showed up. I took off when I saw them grabbing people, hauling them away on the backs of those ATV looking things."

"Did you see anything other than the wheeled robots?" Matt paused in his walking.

"Yeah. I saw this big and tall armored guy. He, or she or it, seemed to be directing those wheeled guys. The Armored guy helped to secure bodies on the back of the six-wheelers."

"Bodies?" James asked.

"Yes, bodies. They weren't moving. I think I saw blood on some."

Janice shivered. James stared out into space.

"Your folks..."

"Taken. As we escaped," stated James. Janice began to cry. Her brother put his arm around her.

"Hey, sorry, Didn't mean to make things worse."

"It is what it is, Matt. We should walk." James took his arm from around Janice and began walking, staring straight ahead. Matt looked questioning at Janice as she wiped her eyes.

"I'll explain later," she whispered to him.

A half-hour later James abruptly stopped and turned to Matt.

"Those tall beings. Robots?" asked James.

"I don't think so. The big guys looked like... huge men in armor. About seven feet tall. They did not act like robots. They acted, moved almost... human." Matt paused, then continued. "At the Buck Creek Campsite, a guy took a shot with a twelve gauge at one of the big guys. The shot bounced off. The big guy took out this sickle-looking object and cut the man who shot him in half with one swipe. No real blood. It was like the wounds were cauterized." He looked at Janice,

"I took off after that, Janice. Low crawled for almost an

hour."

"Laser. Or energized metal would do that," James opined.

"Whatever they had, I hid like a rabbit from a coyote. I found a car with keys in it and hid inside while I listened to the car radio. That's where I heard on an EBS that some humans may be helping the aliens, some kind of renegade group, or groups."

"Not just thugs like tried to rob us?" asked Janice. "My Dad stopped them, got us away."

Matt hesitated as if choosing his words.

"Harvesting. Someone said the aliens and their helpers, the robots, were... hunting humans. Harvesting us like wild cattle, or deer."

"Or pigs," said James. "Human flesh resembles porcine flesh to a high degree."

"Stop it!" yelled Janice. "Don't talk like that, James. Mom and Dad were *not* pigs." She glared at Matt. "Why do you have to spread all those crappy rumors? Huh? Are you saying our poor parents were just slabs of meat?"

"Bacon." James comment was monotone as if he were a machine. Janice stepped up to him and slugged him in the chest. Hard. James stepped back, looked at his sister with a confused look. "Why?"

"Goddamn it, shut up! You talk like a freaking robot yourself. Flip that switch, or hook that loose wire in your head back up. Act like a human brother. Not a soulless piece of crap." Janice's chin was quivering as she ranted. Then she burst into tears.

"Sister, I'm sorry," said James. "You know me. I speak without thinking sometimes. I'm sorry."

"Stop it!" Janice cried out. "Stop apologizing. Like Dad used to say. Step up, rise to the occasion. Or go away, and leave me alone."

Janice pulled a napkin from her pocket and blew her nose on it, stuffed it in her pack. She wiped her eyes with her shirt sleeve, then noticed Matt staring.

"Never seen a woman cry before?" Janice asked.

"Yeah Just never saw one blow snot and stick it her pack before. Saving it?"

Janice stared at him for a moment, then began to laugh. "Yeah. Gonna make a snot ball and throw it at those freaking aliens if I ever see a live one, not a robot." Janice pulled a scrunchy from out of a pocket and used it to tie her hair back in a ponytail. "Should've grabbed a baseball cap for my head."

Matt looked at James. "You okay, Man?" he asked.

"Yes, Matt. But I am different. That confuses and angers people sometimes," James said bluntly.

"Hey, we're all different, James. Some Indian Tribes used to name people based on those differences. But they were family nonetheless."

"You're smart, Matt," stated Janice.

"I try to be. I graduate from High School this year. Or at least take the GED exam. I'm homeschooled."

"Why?" asked James.

"My people said I and others needed to learn more about the old ways," replied Matt. He shrugged. "I guess that has merit. We need to know who and where we came from."

"Some people said I should be homeschooled," said James. "My condition made them feel uncomfortable, they thought I would disrupt things. Father refused." He looked at Matt. "I miss Father. He would know what to do."

Janice walked over and hugged her brother. "Sorry I was so mad. I need more patience, like Mom, always said."

Matt turned and looked back up the trail.

"I think we need to move. I keep getting this feeling between my shoulder blades that someone is looking for us."

"Or *something*," added Janice. "Let's go, then." The three young humans started walking again, headed they hoped was away from danger and toward safety. They all knew that only time would tell.

The three healthy young people made good time. As the walked, Matt, told them in a low voice what to expect.

"This trail will follow the small gorge Buck Creek cut. Then, about after thirty miles of walking, we'll hit an improved trail, the Pacific Coast National Scenic Trail is the fancy name. We head southwest down the train, and we'll hit Highway 2, that goes through Stevens Pass."

"Think it will be okay to walk along the highway by then?" asked Janice. Matt shrugged.

"We'll soon find out," he replied. "If we find a bunch of traffic fleeing to the East, we will know what direction is probably safe. If not..."

"We pick another direction," said James.

"Yes, Sir. We are coming up on the end of the second day. It will be Day Four or Five by the time we hit the highway on foot. If we come across motor transport, it will be different."

"The Scenic Trail, do vehicles use it?" asked Janice.

"Emergency vehicles will. Sometimes a motorbike or an ATV will use it for a while, although the Park Rangers don't like that. It is supposed to be a foot, bike, or horse trail."

"Pristine wilderness, right?" said Janice.

"Yeah, right." Matt snorted as he continued. "Bunch of tourists who spend three hundred an fifty-five days sleeping in a soft bed come up here for a week to ten days and try to walk the trail. A few hardcore Through-Hikers show up, but they are rare."

"Through-Hikers?" James asked.

"The real serious ones. They start down in California, hike all the way up. The pros start at the Mexican U.S. Border and try to make it all the way to the Canadian Border. On foot, those are few and far between."

"We'll make it. We won't slow you down," stated James. Matt examined him closely.

"Yeah, James," Matt said. "You strike me as the type that once you put your mind to it, you finish what you started." Janice laughed.

"You don't know the half of it, Matt."

Hours later, Matt looked at the setting sun. The alien Deltas had stopped flying over, which meant the trio could walk without diving into the brush anytime they heard them. Whether they were reconnaissance aircraft or not, the young people did not want the chance of being seen. Without communications with the outside, they did not know what other steps the invaders were taking.

"Follow me, please," requested Matt. "We'll make camp close to the creek so we'll have fresh water."

"Think anybody will come down the creek?" Janice asked.

"I doubt it," replied Matt. "Anybody trying to catch up would have been heard by us by now."

They made camp and Matt started to put together a fire, with James help. Janice checked the food supplies. The trio had shared just a sandwich on the way, trying not to stop nor to use up the food supplies. Janice laid out three sandwiches and water bottles. After the fire was going, Matt went down to the creek and filled his canteen, the one item he had from his original camp along with his rifle. The three sat on logs and prepared to each their limited repast.

"Think a prayer would be in order?" Janice asked.

"Why not?" answered Matt Bearclaw. "We need all the help we can get."

"Could you do it?" asked James. "I would like to hear an Indian prayer."

"Okay, no problem."

Matt bent closer to the fire, closed his eyes and used his cupped hands to draw some of the smoke towards him. Janice and James followed his lead and closed their eyes.

"Great Spirit," Matt deep voice intoned. "Grant us your strength to fight the evil that has come to your land, your mountains, and forests. Give us your protection as we deal with these Evil Ones, fight to preserve your Earth. Help us to honor those were lost. We ask for your blessings. Thank You."

"Amen," said Janice.

"Is that a traditional prayer, Matt?" James asked.

"Nope. I let the Great Spirit guide me to the words."

"That was very nice. Thank you," Janice said.

They had soon finished their meal and readied for sleep.

"Now, I'll take your blanket if I may, you two use your sleeping bags," Matt said.

"We could hook the two bags together, and we all sleep in one bed," James stated

"Nope. It's not that cold yet. I'm used to it. I'm tougher than you Whiteeyes, as all those bad Westerns my Dad watched would say."

The three new friends laughed and were soon in their

respective beds. As they settled in for the night, the campfire allowed to burn down, Janice called out.

"Goodnight, Johnboy,"

"Sister there is no John here."

"Someday, Brother, you will have a sense of humor."

"When my Sister can tell a joke, I will laugh."

"Yeah, sure James. By the way, love ya."

"And I you, Janice. Matt, goodnight. And... thank you."

"Anytime, James. Anytime."

The Sun woke up the trio. They saw to their toilet, shared a sandwich three ways for light breakfast, and broke camp. Matt looked at James' bow and arrows.

"These target arrows can still take a deer down if you hit it in the right place. They're not broad tip hunting arrows, but they'll do."

"I have a pistol in my pack, but no bullets," offered James.

"Let me see it, please." Matt took the pistol, worked the slide and checked the chamber.

"Nine millimeter. We should find some shells for this someplace along the way."

"You still have shells for your rifle?" Janice asked.

"About a dozen. I'll try to save the ammunition for any of those dammed robots. A .44 Magnum seems to make nice big holes in them."

They were up and hiking in some five minutes. Matt watched his two new friends with appreciation. They had not been overly stiff from the night out, did not grump and complain when they had to get up and hike again. Matt knew he could have done a hundred times worse for companions during a Space Alien Invasion. Thus, the three made good time. The forest and game trails they followed were not too overgrown.

By noon they reached the Pacific Crest National Scenic Trail. And, met the first humans outside of their small group.

Clumped around a pickup truck sporting the National Forest Service symbol were some dozen people and two horses. They seemed to be throwing questions and statements at the young woman wearing a Forest Service green uniform. The three young adults cautiously approached as they could tell there was a high degree of emotion among the people.

"What the hell is happening?" a large man with a beard and backpack was saying in a loud voice. The young Forest Service employee held her hands up in the form of supplication.

"Sir, I told you everything I know. The Emergency Broadcast System says there numerous areas of destruction, fires, and disorder thanks to the meteors. There are also reports of strange aircraft…"

"Strange?" A middle-aged man with a handlebar mustache jumped in. "A big-ass flying ark shook the ground and scared our horses last night. It sure wasn't an airplane I have ever seen before." His blonde horse-riding companion nodded her head in agreement.

"Please, everyone," the U.S. Forest Service employee tried to continue. "I'm not an Enforcement Forest Ranger. I do seasonal work around the main Ranger Station. I was sent up this trail as I was the only person free to come here."

"What good are you then?" sneered a red-headed college-age female with a backpack and two other female hiker friends.

"Hey, give her a chance!" yelled Janice. "We're all in the same boat out here."

"Oh, yeah?" said the red-head. "So what do you know, smartass?"

"She knows that aliens have attacked and killed people." James comment shut everyone up as they turned to stare at him.

"Excuse me. I'm Forest Officer Sally Card," the Forest

Service employee said as she tried to take control. "What did you just say?"

"My friend James just said what we saw," Matt interjected. "Darrington and tribal lands are overrun with wheeled robots that came out of some large alien spacecraft we all saw. Believe us or don't believe us, we don't care. We're headed to Stevens Pass and then Eastern Washington. Western Washington is a disaster area." The dozen hikers and riders froze, then looked at each other. Someone from the back of the group yelled out "You're nuts!" Matt shrugged, turned to Officer Card.

"You offering rides down to Highway Two?"

"Why yes. That is why I was sent here. To round up as many people as I can and get them down to the Pass Highway. We have First Responder units forming there."

"Shall we?" asked Matt as he looked at his new friends.

"Riding is better than walking," answered Janice. The young trio moved towards the pickup truck as the small crowd began to argue among itself. A couple of the men including the bearded one with the backpack advanced on the Forest Service employee.

"No one leaves until we have some answers," the Bearded One bellowed.

"Leave her alone," said Janice as she stepped in between them and Sally Card. The sizeable bearded male shoved her back, yelling.

James seemed to come from nowhere. He shoved the barrel of the empty pistol into the side of the Beared One's sizable head. Of course, the man did not know the gun was empty. So he froze.

"Don't touch my sister," James spoke in a cold and monotone voice that got everyone's attention without yelling. Matt stepped up, his rifle ready in his hands.

"You want trouble? Keep this up, and you'll get trouble, Either from us, or those... things that are killing people and taking them away for God knows what.”

"Taking them?" the blonde horsewoman asked. "Why?"

"As I said, we don't know," replied Matt. He turned to Sally Card. "Can we leave, Ma'am?"

"Yes," Sally answered. The young employee turned to the group. "I can squeeze in about a half a dozen more." The group kept arguing as the Bearded One stepped back, his face pale.

"We'll follow along behind you," the two horseriders called out. At the last moment, a young couple who had been staying in the background strode up the truck and threw their packs in, then clambered in after them.

"All aboard," Sally called out as she started the truck. Janice was squeezed in the truck bed with James, who seemed unnaturally calm after threatening to shot a man.

"You had no bullets," Janice whispered to James.

"I know. He didn't," replied her brother. Janice chuckled and looped her arm through his, then looked closely at him and frowned.

"Would you have shot him if you had to?"

"No one hurts my family," James answered with no emotion.

Matt took the 'shotgun' seat with the Forest Service Employee. He looked back and laughed.

"Something funny?" Sally asked as she slowly drove down the Pacific Coast Trail.

"They're still arguing back there, rather than head down to where there are people who can help them."

"They don't realize they need help, Mister…"

"Matt, Ma'am."

"Sally," the young woman said as she stuck out her hand for a shake. Just then the area was shaken by a sonic boom. Sally let out a surprised yelp.

"What was that?" said Sally.

"Sonic Boom," James yelled from the back. "From a

Delta."

"Delta? What's that? One of our aircraft?"

"No Sally," replied Matt. "We told all of you. Aliens. Real, live UFOs."

"Oh, shit," the Forest Service employee said. She began to drive the pickup faster, which was not easy on the narrow trail.

Matt stuck his head out the passenger side window and tried to scan the sky. He looked back and saw the two horseriders were in a fast trot to try and keep up. The trot then turned into a canter as they tried to catch up. Next, it became a gallop. Sally was trying to maneuver past some overhanging branches when there was a loud explosion from the area where the group of 'stay-behinds,' remained.

"That was not another sonic boom," Sally informed Matt.

"No, it was not. Pull over among the next clump of trees you can fit the truck in."

Some ten seconds later the truck was partially hidden under the boughs of some old growth Douglas Firs. The two horse riders caught up and dismounted next to the pickup. Janice had just found out the young couple in the back was newlyweds on an adventurous honeymoon when their conversation was interrupted by the sonic boom. As soon as Sally stopped the truck, the two newlyweds had a hushed conversation, then hopped out of the back of the pickup. They grabbed their packs and headed into the brush.

"Hey," Janice called after them. "Why are you leaving?"

"That pickup is too big of a target," the man called back. He waved, then they disappeared behind some trees.

"Based on his haircut and demeanor, I think he is Military," James told his sister.

"I didn't even get their names," complained Janice.

Matt exited the pickup and stepped slowly out onto the trail. The horserider couple was under trees on the other side of the pathway. Sally handed Matt some binoculars, and he looked back towards from whence they came. He noticed a plume of smoke rising from the area the group had been in. As Matt trained the binoculars on the trail towards the plume of smoke, he saw a solitary figure in a stumbling run towards them.

"I think the group got shelled. Or bombed," Matt said to Sally.

"Should we move?" she asked him.

"Not yet. We need to see what's going to happen next."

They got their answer. There was a feeling of electricity in the air followed by a low humming sound which was felt in their bones as well as heard. From what seemed like nowhere, a massive disk-shaped craft appeared over the running figure. Matt, Sally, James, and Janice all crouched in and around the pickup, hoping the occupants of the 'flying saucer' would not notice them. But then they saw the subject of the craft's attention. What looked from a distance like a long metallic tentacle shot out from the flying disc at the stumbling figure. One second the human was on the trail, the next second it was yanked into the bowels of the alien craft. The next moment, the disc was zipping straight up out of sight. The four humans at the truck stayed still, shocked into immobility. Finally, Matt spoke.

"That... thing looks like something Hans Solo would fly."

"It's quite similar," James opinionated.

Across the pathway, the two riders took off down the trail at full gallop.

"Hope they don't hit a branch," said Sally.

"That is the least of their worries," Matt said. "That Delta may still be around. I think it shot at the group, and that disc craft cleaned up the mess."

"Meat," stated James.

"What?" Janice asked.

"Meat. That explains what the aliens are all doing. The wheeled robots, those... Robocops you saw. Now that disc. The only reason they are taking the dead and injured are for meat. Food."

The other three humans were stunned into silence by the observations of James Then, Janice began to cry. Then to yell.

"You slimy sonsabitches," she yelled between her sobs. "You think you can eat my family and get away with it?" The furious young lady picked up rocks and began to throw them in the direction of the smoke plume. James walked up and hugged his sister.

"Sister, we must go. Mother and Father would want us to be safe."

Janice hugged her brother. They separated. Sally gave Janice some tissues to wipe her eyes and nose.

"I think its time to move on," said Sally. Matt nodded his head 'yes.'

Janice nodded. "Okay."

Janice and James climbed into the back of the pickup, as Matt reoccupied the 'shotgun' seat. Matt handed the binoculars to James to keep a lookout for any Alien Craft. Sally started the truck and slowly pulled back out onto the trail. She slowly accelerated the vehicle.

"How far do we have to go to hit the Highway?" Matt asked.

"About thirty-five miles," replied the Forest Service employee. "It'll take a while as you can tell that this pathway is not built wide for vehicles. It is supposed to be a hiking or horseback trail."

"What does the Forest Service do if there was a serious medical emergency?" Matt asked.

"We have access to medical response helicopters," Sally replied. "I think all out air assets were caught on the ground, by the meteorites or the fire. Or maybe those Deltas you mentioned."

"Well, maybe we'll find some help once we reach Highway 2 and Stevens Pass," said Matt.

Sally tried to keep the pickup moving between twenty-five and thirty miles per hour. Again when they neared areas where the Douglas Fir and other trees encroached on the trail, Sally had to slow down. She did not want to risk damaging the truck by hitting a tree root or branch. Some twenty minutes of traveling down the trail and they caught up with the two horseriders. The man and woman were in a clearing by the pathway, looked as if they were checking the hooves and shoes of their mounts.

"Well," said Matt. "At least they didn't hit a tree and break their—"

Two hypervelocity objects smashed into the riders and mounts. The impact force tore the horses into pieces and bloody chunks. The two humans were propelled out into the clearing as a loud sonic crack from the projectiles reverberated around the clearing and the surrounding trees.

"*Delta!*" James cried out from the bed of the truck.

"Into the brush, now," Matt told Sally. She cranked the steering wheel and forced the vehicle in between two large evergreen trees. Sally slammed on the brakes, put the truck into park and leapt from the cab as Matt jumped from the passenger side. Janice and James bailed from the truck bed and landed in some brush next to Matt. Sally scrambled and joined the three friends. She shook and blinked back tears.

"What was that?" Sally blurted out.

"I saw two bright flashes in the sky miles behind us," answered James. "A Delta must have fired some weapon at the horses."

"My God, from miles away, out of sight?" Janice asked.

"Some kind of projectile weapon," said James.

"If so, that is one hell of an aircraft gun," said Matt. "Miles away and pinpoint accuracy. Does our military have anything like that?"

"Maybe the 30MM A-10 Thunderbolt II anti-armor weapon. But just two rounds? The A- 10s gun is a powered Gatling, It can't just fire two rounds like what happened," explained James.

Sally stood up from the brush in which she hid. The Forest Service employee started to walk towards where the two people were in the clearing. Matt grabbed her and pulled her back.

"No! Wait." Matt walked her into the shadow of a large Douglas Fir.

"Remember what happened after that last attack on the group? That flying disc appeared and grabbed that guy trying to get away."

"But we can't just leave them there, Matt. They may still be alive."

"Just wait, please," answered Matt. "If it is like last time, it should just be a couple of minutes."

No sooner had he answered that they felt the same electrified atmosphere as if someone was discharging a massive battery into the air. Next came the humming which seemed to penetrate them to their core. The flying elongated disc zipped into the airspace above where the two horseriders had been knocked. Again, tentacles darted down from the alien craft and snatched the humans from the ground. Matt could not tell if they were still alive or not. If they were, he thought, they probably would not be for long.

Sally began to shake and tremble again.

"I want to go home," she said. "I never agreed to all of this. I just wanted a summer job. I'm supposed to go back to college next week."

"Janice," said Matt. "Can you stay here with Sally?" I'm going to go examine all that horse meat."

"I'll keep a lookout with the binoculars," said James. Matt made quick time to the equine remains. There were no signs of cauterization as there had been with the weapon used by what James named a Robocop at the Buck Creek campsite. Some bullet or shell traveling at a very high velocity had torn the two horses asunder with pure kinetic energy. Matt bent over, pulled out his hunting knife, and sliced several steaks from what was left of the hindquarters of one horse. One saddlebag was still in good shape, so he confiscated it to hold the fresh meat. Matt was pleasantly surprised as he found a full-sized Berretta nine millimeter pistol in the bag, with a small box of shells. He stuck the gun on his belt and the ammo box in his jacket pocket. There was a plastic garbage bag in the saddle bag also, so he used it to hold the meat. He also found a full water bottle which went into one of his pockets, as did several protein bars he found. Then he ran back to where his companions were hidden.

"Come on. Now we go. I have some steaks for later."

"Horse meat?" asked Janice.

"Sure, why not?" answered Matt. "We didn't kill them. Coyotes and other critters will clean up the rest."

"I always wondered what horse tasted like," James stated.

"Sally, can we leave now?" asked Matt. The young lady took a deep breath.

"Yes, why not? There's no one else here." Within five minutes, they were back in the truck and headed to the Stevens Pass Highway. Matt had Janice ride shotgun with Sally to try and keep her focused. In the bed of the pickup, he watched James load the empty pistol his Father had taken from the neighbor in what seemed like ages ago.

"You know how to handle that thing," Matt commented.

"Uncle Mark showed me how to shoot. He is a Survivalist. That's what my Mother calls him." James paused, then added, "Did call him. I guess they are both... gone." He looked Matt in the eyes. "And the next question is, in my so-called condition, can I use it."

"That is a question," stated Matt.

"As I told Janice," replied James. "No one hurts my

family, my sister."

"You seem pretty focused, James. Why do people seem to think you have a problem?"

James paused for a moment before answering. "Because, Matt, at times I do have a problem around people. I have trouble reading what is appropriate in social situations. But only sometimes. As my Father said when he tried to explain. It is like I have a loose wire as if a neuron fires wrong as it flops around someplace in my head. None of the Doctors could explain it any better. Some said I was too focused, others said I focused on the wrong things, some that I had trouble focusing day to day, period." James made a raspberry sound, which caused Matt to laugh.

"That is what I say, Matt, short for Matthew, yes? I am 'me.' As long as I do not hurt someone, beyond making them a bit frustrated, why should anyone care? I will not be a burden on anyone. I will work and live." James frowned for a moment. "That is if these aliens do not eat me. They ignored the slaughter horseflesh, so I believe that shows who and what they find tasty."

"So you think they are here to 'harvest' us James?"

"There is just no other answer when you analyze the situation. The aliens grab alive and dead humans, make no attempt to ask us to surrender that anyone has reported, seemed to be organized to find us and hunt us down. Like you would do a deer, Matt."

Matt sat for a moment looking at James. Then he grinned and clapped James on his back.

"You just keep analyzing, friend. You're good at it. You may save us all." James smiled back.

"I like you as a friend, Matt. Thank you for being my friend. Sometimes that can be hard."

"Hell, James," Matt responded. "Real friendship has it's ups and down. That is the human condition." Matt knocked on the truck roof, then called out through Janice's open vehicle window.

"You ladies hungry?"

"Not if it's that horsemeat, Matt."

"Naw. Some protein bars I scrounged. What say you?"

"Sure, why not?" Janice replied.

Sally seemed to have regained some of her composure as she drove the pickup at a slow and steady pace. Sally maneuvered around natural barriers in those areas where the forest had tried to reclaim the trail. The four companions made some small talk as they traveled, mostly about their past. Most of the time they sat quiet, scanning the sky and forest areas for Alien craft and six-wheeled vehicles. Sally's steady driving resulted in them reaching the intersection of the Pacific Crest Natural Scenic Trail and Highway 2 at Stevens Pass as the Sun was beginning to set. At the junction of the trail and the roadway, the four young humans saw the first large-scale effects of the apparent attack and invasion.

As Sally drove the pickup up onto the roadway, the four companions could see some hundred vehicles trying to weave their way around at least a dozen wrecked and/or burnt motor vehicles.

"My God," said Sally.

"I take it this was not the scene when you left this place," stated Janice

"No, it was not, When Ranger Bob sent me up the trail to look for people, there was like a half a dozen cars stopped and asked him what was going on. That's it. And look at that plume of black smoke. That looks like it is coming from near the ski lodges."

Someone yelled Sally's name. A man wearing a Forest Rangers uniform and badge, with a gun belt around his waist strode up to the pickup truck. He grinned as he walked up and put his hand on Sally's arm.

"Am I glad to see you! I was afraid you weren't coming back. And I see you brought some people back with you."

"Matt, Janice, James, this is Ranger Bob Paterson. He tries to keep all of the seasonal and summer help out of trouble." They exchanged greetings, then the Forest Rangers face changed to a worried look.

"Some... things flew by and strafed the cars headed through Stevens Pass. This is the result."

"Deltas," stated James.

"What?" said Ranger Bob.

"Those aircraft, we ran into them the second day after the rocks from space hit," explained Janice. "We've been dodging them ever since.

The four young companions gave the Ranger a quick and dirty review of the death and destruction they had seen. As they finished, the Forest Ranger stood silent for a full minute before he spoke.

"I have a State Trooper and a young National Guard Private helping me sort out this mess. We tried radioing for help, but everything is confused. No one seems to be in charge right now, not even the President."

"No President?" asked James.

"The last report is the Vice President is in D.C. and is in charge."

"That's Lisa what's-her-name," said Janice. Matt snorted.

"My Dad and Uncle said she was chosen during the last election for eye candy," he said.

"Why, because she's female?" Janice said defensively.

"No, because she has little real experience and has a nice body."

"Be that as it may," the Ranger interrupted, " she is still the Acting Commander In Chief."

"Has she said anything to us?" Asked James. The Ranger shrugged as he replied.

"Just that she and others were working to get the situation in hand."

"That is not very comforting," stated Sally. Just then,

there was a short burst of a siren. The Ranger looked down the Highway.

"Our State Trooper has returned."

A few moments later and a Washington State Patrol vehicle pulled up next to the small group and stopped. A good-sized light-skinned woman who was not a spring chicken stepped from the car and walked to the five humans.

"I see Miss Card located some people on the trail," said the woman in the Smokey Bear Hat.

"This is Sergeant Mandy Moriarty. Sergeant, this is James and Janice Richards, brother and sister. The other young man is Matt Bearclaw.'

"Which tribe?" the Sergeant asked Matt.

"Salish Puyallup. Came down from Darrington," replied Matt. "And to answer your next question, the area is overrun with space aliens."

"So it's true. This is an invasion, pure and simple," said Sgt. Moriarty.

"More than that," James chimed in. "They are harvesting us."

"How do you know that, young man?" asked the Sergeant.

"Because I analyzed what I saw, Ma'am."

There was a pause in the conversation as the State Trooper seemed to digest what had just been said. She looked at Sally Card.

"You saw the action also, Sally?"

"Yes, Sergeant," replied Sally with a shake in her voice. "People, both dead and alive, were picked up by those large disc-shaped craft. Everything else was ignored. James' analysis fits."

"Shit," said the Trooper. "Well, they, whoever they are, blasted the hell out the parts of this highway. And we have not found any bodies in the cars and trucks hit by the alien weapons.

So yeah, it fits." The Sergeant adjusted her gun belt and dressed Sally Card again,

"So, you want to make another trip..."

"Sergeant, the ones left behind are either dead or in the deep forest, hiding," interjected Matt. "All it will do is make her a target again."

"Double shit," replied Moriarty. "Okay, Sally. Head west over the Pass. Last partial message I got was that forces are regrouping at Fairchild Air Force Base in Spokane. Joint Base Lewis-McChord is toast. Ships in the ports and at Bangor Submarine Base are being hit with underwater mines carried by... something. End of the third day and we still do not have a good picture of the enemy."

"Mind if we scrounge for food and supplies, Sergeant?" asked Matt.

"Go ahead," Moriarty replied. "Just no fighting. I see you're armed. Don't misuse your firepower. Share what you get with others."

"Yes, Ma'am."

The four companions remounted the pickup and Sally drove west. "We'll check around the ski lodges, chalets. People may have stores stuff in them. We can leave I.O. Us for anything we take." The four knew that was fantasy talking as none of them even had a viable contact address. But the imagination made them feel more honest. Sally drove to the large parking areas around the ski area. They found a couple of cars with full open doors, keys in the ignition with no owners around.

"They either ran or were taken," James matter-of-factly stated as they approached the first vehicle. The four used the keys in both cars to open the trunks. They found some snacks, water, a loaf of bread and some butter. Matt pulled out a fifth of bourbon out of the second car.

"You going to keep that?" asked Janice.

"Medicinal use, of course," answered Matt. "Dump it on an open wound, it kills germs."

The four companions soon found other open vehicles, as well as the source of the massive plume of dark smoke. A tanker truck full of gasoline had been hit by something and set ablaze. Sally started to maneuver the pickup around the hazard towards the ski lodges when Matt pointed something out.

"Look at all those people looking at us through those picture windows," Matt said. "I don't think those people will take kindly to us trying to intrude on their buildings."

"Why?" asked James. "The Sergeant said people should share."

"James, judging by their facial expressions, I don't think they got the memo."

Sally drove the pickup further up the highway until they saw an SUV with a ten-gallon jerrycan strapped over its spare tire, She quickly pulled over behind it, and Matt jumped out of the truck. He made a beeline to the gas can and cut the straps with his hunting knife. Matt grabbed and carried the jerrycan back to the pickup.

"Feels like a full ten gallons," opined Matt. "Now, look for some clothes, underwear in the next cars we check. We are going to start getting ripe.."

The companions soon found a mishmash of clothes in three successive vehicles. In twenty minutes they were back on the road.

"We have a half of tank. That should get us to Leavenworth without using the jerrycan," Matt said.

"Think we should find a place to bed down?" asked Sally.

"Not yet," answered Matt. "Let's see if we can find a way to get to Leavenworth first."

ally drove at a steady pace on Highway 2. The companions passed a serious of empty cars and trucks. There were no indicators as to where the occupants had gone. Sally kept driving. Approximately an hour later they entered the city limits of Leavenworth. The European Alpine in appearance tourist destination no longer had that beautiful and happy appearance. Instead, clumps of motor vehicles and people were spread all over the various roads, streets and parking lots. Some seemed to be arguing, others just seemed to be standing or sitting, waiting. But one fact was readily observable. There were few First Responder vehicles or personnel.

"Should we find a place to stay?" Sally asked.

"No," said Matt. "There are way too many people hanging around for the resources. I bet you people who were in the local hotels, bed, and breakfasts, and campgrounds are not moving. Not to mention tempers are on edge."

"Where to then?"

"Cashmere is next. If we have to, we'll camp out in the nearby brush."

Down the road, they went, as the Sun moved down behind the mountains. It was turning dark as they entered the small town of Cashmere.

Sally slowed the pickup to about five miles an hour. There were no street lights, no store lights, no electric lights at all.

"This does not look good," Janice said. Sally stopped the pickup.

"I'll lead the way on foot," stated Matt as he climbed out of the truck bed.

"I'll help," added James.

The two young men slowly walked down the middle of the road, looking for any sign of life. A sudden running dog made the four humans jump. They continued, the truck lights the only illumination in the town. Still, no humans appeared.

"This is spooky," Matt said.

"The people are just hiding," said James. "That is a normal human reaction. They are just terrified. Like during the Orson Wells broadcast."

"Huh? I don't get it, James."

"Just before World War Two, Orson Wells produced that War of the Worlds radio broadcast. A lot of people thought the Martians were invading."

"Oh, I remember now," said Matthew. "Concrete, Washington. I guess a bunch of those people ran into the hills."

"Exactly," replied James.

A loud voice came from the dark.

"Shut those headlights off and get off the highway," an unknown male yelled. "They'll come back."

"Who are 'they'?" Asked Matt.

"Just get off the goddammed road. Otherwise, we'll shoot your headlights out."

Sally shut the truck lights out and stopped the vehicle.

"Matt, this looks bad," said Janice.

"Well, we can't stay in the middle of the highway. And I find it hard to believe there are no cops or military around. Where are they?"

"They were sent towards those landing Arks people have mentioned," said James. "They're massive, they came after all the destruction and fires. So anyone not initially responding to those areas would be sent towards these aforementioned flying Arks."

"But are those Arks the 'they,' James?"

Before James could answer, the four companions all heard a horribly familiar sound. A loud electric hum from the motor of an Alien six-wheeled robot came from behind them.

"James! Jump in the back. Sally, take off!" Matt commanded as he scrambled into the pickup bed. Sally started the pickup, gunned the engine and slammed it into gear. As the vehicle accelerated thanks to Sally's heavy foot on the gas pedal, something slammed into the pickup tailgate. Janice cried out, turned in the shotgun seat and saw what had hit the pickup. An alien land harpoon had penetrated halfway through the tailgate. Janice screamed a warning as the rear of the truck suddenly jerked around, then the tailgate was ripped from the pickup. Sally managed to straighten the vehicle's path, and stomped on the accelerator again.

"How fast can they go, James?" Janice yelled out.

"How do I know, Sister? I didn't build them."

"Analyze them, dammit. Analyze!" Janice shouted at him.

"I am not 'Data' from Star Trek, Janice."

A bright floodlight lit up the pickup, as well as seared the two humans in the bed. Matt let out a yell, then pointed his rifle and fired at the light. As much due to luck as to skill, the .44 Magnum round hit the center of the bright floodlight, and it winked out. Sally turned the truck headlights on as the pickup accelerated to over sixty miles an hour. James and Matt blinked their eyes and tried to see through the gloom.

"Is it still back there?" Janice yelled back.

"We can't tell," James yelled back.

"We're going to hit Sunnyslope next, then Wenatchee and the upper Columbia River," Sally yelled out over the wind and engine noise.

"Turn north once we cross the Columbia River," directed James as he blinked his eyes to clear them from the results of the spotlight.

"Why?" Sally called back.

"South takes us closer to Hanford. We do not want to be by a nuclear material storage site with space aliens around."

"Yeah. That's right."

Sunnyslope was as blacked out as Cashmere. And as deserted. The group crossed the bridge that spanned the Columbia, and Sally turned the truck north up towards the small town of Orondo.

"Hey, guys. We are getting low on gas," said Sally.

"Pull over, and we'll use the jerrycan," replied Matt. In a couple of minutes, they were stopped and blacked out. Matt grabbed the jerrycan which had luckily not been pulled or knocked out of the pickup bed by the wheeled robot. As Matt field the truck, James stood and stared. Finally, Janice walked up and touched his arm.

"Brother? You with us?"

James jerked, turned his head to look at Janice. He looked at his sister for a couple of moments before answering. "I guess," James finally said. Janice gave him a short hug. Matt finished emptying the jerrycan into the pickup and put it in the truck bed. Sally was looking up the roadway. She turned towards her companions

"I think there is a small State Park a few miles up. I think we need to spend the night there. I don't want to run into any more wheeled robots in the dark."

The other three people readily agreed. They clambered into the pickup and were soon at Lincoln Rock State Park.

Sally drove the blacked out pickup slowly into the park off of Highway 2. There were a couple of parked RVs as well as some tents. She found one of the few cabins in the park and parked in front of it. All four young adults slowly snuck around the cabin, looked through the windows. Janice lightly knocked on the door. There was no answer. She pushed and twisted the doorknob.

"It's locked," Janice said.

"Well, we could break in…" Matt began, then noticed that James was walking up to the door. The young man had what looked like were small and thin strips of wire or metal. James bent over and began some arcane manipulations with the lock. Within a minute, James twisted the doorknob, and it opened.

"Where'd you learn that, James?" his sister asked. James shrugged.

"I couldn't sleep one night. Looked it up on the internet, figured out how to make the picks and shims. Then I played around with locks until I opened them."

"Well, that's nice. I'm dead," stated Sally. "Take what you want from the truck. I am crashing on that sofa."

Twenty minutes later, they had the sleeping bags laid out, and Matt was making a small fire in the campfire pit in the back. When Janice asked him what he was planning to do, he said he wanted some horse steak.

"Now?"

"Why not?" Matt replied. "If those RVs or tents have occupants, they can come over, and I'll share. You want some?"

"I do," said James.

"I'll stick to a remaining sandwich," said Janice. "Sally is sacked out on the couch. I'm going to join her after I wash up. The water seems to be working."

"Suit yourself. James, look for condiments and spices, anything else you want."

"Okay."

A half hour later, and the two young men were pigging out on the horseflesh.

"This is good, Matt. As good as beef."

"Well, my friend, many a horse was eaten by many an Indian on the Great Plains. And a few more here and there on the West Coast."

James finished his goodly portion of the meat, set his plate down and leaned against a log bench. Matt finished his steak and did the same. No one had come over from either the RVs nor the tents. No one wanted to go and check them out for fear of what they may find. They had seen enough death.

"So, tell me, James. What do you think about that robot chasing us? Where are these Arks landing and why?" James sat for a few moments, deep in thought. Then he answered.

"They, the Aliens, have certain spots or areas picked out for...harvesting. I think that is precisely what they are doing, harvesting us. Otherwise, they would be talking to somebody. But to them, we are like cattle. No reasonable person around wants to talk to cows, ask their opinions about us eating them."

"What do you think they look like?" asked Matt.

"I have no idea. I think the Aliens watched our TV broadcasts, listened to our radio transmissions as they seem to know how we operate. But what they look like? Don't know. They do not have to look like their robots or those Robocops you saw."

"Well, my friend James, I for one am hitting the rack. We can do some more figuring in the morning."

"Good idea, Matt. Good idea."

Sometime before sunrise, a loud wopping and thwacking noise woke them. Sally called out "Helicopter!" as she sprang from the couch and to the front door. It took her a few moments to get the door unlocked and opened. Then she stepped out on the front porch and into the ground effect caused by the large blades of the aircraft. Her three companions soon joined her as they tried to make out the large dark rotorcraft that hovered above the campground.

"Sounds like a Blackhawk," Sally said. "Probably military rescue. Grab a flashlight, and we'll let them know—"

Something streaked towards the Blackhawk. A massive explosion lit up the aircraft as the missile hit. Sally screamed as Matt grabbed her and shoved her into the cabin and then down on to the wooden floor. All four people flattened themselves to the cabin floor as best as they could. They heard something smash into the pickup truck. A massive ground impact occurred nearby, and the cabin shook. Next came a large flash and explosion near where the RVs were parked.

Matt peeked a look out the open front door and could only see smoke and flames. He realized some of the smoke was coming from the pickup truck. He untangled himself from Sally and crawled on his hands and knees out onto the porch. The source of the smoke from the pickup truck was a large hunk of aircraft metal which had plowed through the windshield. The metal hunk was still smoldering and in danger of setting the vehicle on fire. He then heard loud human voices coming from beyond the crash site. Sally was suddenly crouched by his side.

"We need to help those people in the 'copter," demanded the Forest Service employee.

"First we need to see what is going on, and stop the truck from burning," Matt replied.

Sally noticed what Matt was talking about, cried out and leapt towards the vehicle. She yanked a fire extinguisher from a rack in the bed and began to spray foam over the smoldering piece of debris. Her aim was accurate, and the fire danger subsided.

Matt, Janice, and James all joined Sally near the truck and surveyed the damage. "Can we drive it?" Janice asked.

As she spoke, a rough voice from out of the darkness yelled. "Hands up, assholes!"

Several rough looking individuals appeared in a semi-circle around them. James looked at the new arrivals.

"You are not military from the helicopter," he said to no one in particular.

"No shit, Sherlock," the original voice said. "Now, hands up!"

"Hey, what do you think—" Janice never finished the statement as a figure came out of the darkness and knocked her down.

"Shut up!" the foul-smelling man yelled at her.

"Hey, Man—" Matt's sentence was never finished as a gun barrel was jammed in his face. Six figures, five males, and one female—all needing baths and clean clothes—were now seen in the ambient light of the fires around them. They were armed within an eclectic array of firearms. The foul-smelling man with the voice acted like he was in charge as he barked out orders to the others.

"Bob, Harry, go check around the 'copter for survivors. Bring me at least one."

A disrepute pair broke off from the semi-circle and headed towards the wrecked aircraft. Mr. Smelly walked up to Sally.

"Forest Service huh? Anymore around?"

"I don't know," answered Sally. "We were just resting, Mister..."

"You can call me Jay. Mister Jay. It has a nice ring to it, don't ya think?" The other three remaining malcontents laughed at their Boss' comment.

"You shot down the Blackhawk," James spoke in a monotone.

"James…" said Janice.

The man called Jay walked over to James.

"Well, James. Look at the brain on you! Figured that out all by yourself."

"Why?" James asked. "Why help the Aliens?"

"Damn! Look, people. We have a genius here. Figured out some of us may not like the people running things, might want a change. Especially if 'change' pays well. Real well."

Jay shifted his attention to Janice. "And aren't you the sweet thing. See, this deal we worked out with a guy we called Mister Strange also states we get access to certain fringe benefits. Meaning, any strange pussy we come across." As he finished speaking, he reached his hand up to touch Janice, and she slapped it away.

"Oh, feisty, aren't we?" Jay stepped back, pulled out a collapsible baton and deployed it. A series of gunshots drew the groups attention.

"Sue," ordered Jay. "Go and check that out."

"Right, Boss."

"There will be a slight delay in the play as we deal with more pressing problems," Jay said as he looked at Janice. "But we will resume action at the next opportunity."

Sue came out of the darkness followed by Bob and Harry. They had suspended between them a figure in full Battle Rattle, minus a weapon. The dumped the character in front of Jay. The Boss used a small flashlight to examine the person on the ground. The was wet blood on the left combat fatigue pants leg.

"Get that light out of my eyes, *pendejo*," the female servicemember growled at Jay, which prompted a cuff from Bob to her head. He cursed as he forgot she still had her Fritz helmet on.

"Brilliant, Buddy. Top of your class in daycare last week," the woman said. Bod started to kick he when Jay motioned him to stop.

"Tough girl, huh? You a dyke? A big tough deisel dyke?"

Jay's comment prompted a round of laughter. The servicewoman chuckled as she removed her helmet. The four companions saw a mid-twenties Hispanic women, her jet black hair tied back in tight braids.

She set her helmet down and looked up at Jay. "You know. If I were a dyke, I'd have a strap-on with your name on it. Just as you like it."

The smile disappeared from Jay's face. He raised his metal baton as the Latina woman sneered at him.

"You can't do that." It was James again. All of the malcontents stopped and looked at him.

"And why the hell not, brainiac?" asked Jay. "You gonna stop me?"

"She is a Non-Commissioned Officer. She deserves respect," added James.

"Staff Sergeant Camila Sanchez at your service," interjected the woman. "Late of USAF Pararescue out of McChord Air Force Base. The young man saw my stripes. These other *putos* must be blind."

"You think your stripes are gonna save you, bitch?" sneered Jay. "Bob, Harry, I think we need a break. Take her inside this cabin, find something for a bed. Have fun." He turned back to Janice. "You're next, sweet cakes. Then the Forest Service. Might as well enjoy our fringe benefits when we can."

"Is all this necessary?" asked Matt. "We're all pieces of meat to a certain type of aliens we haven't even seen yet."

Jay guffawed. "Show how much you know. Yeah, see this?" He held up an object that looked like a cellular telephone as he spoke. "I dial a certain code on this little communicator Mr. Strange gave me and, ZIP! One of those oversized flying saucers shows up, cleans up all the flesh and blood we provide. Do another code and, ZAP! Things get blown up by those Deltas. Or finally, ZIPZAPZIP! And those humongous harvester Arks come down, start taking everything on two legs, dead and alive." Jay displayed an evil grin.

"Mr. Strange, we call him that because he looks kinda Human. But his eyes, the slope of his skull just isn't... right. So he's an alien, but not the ones in charge. Whatever. I don't care. These aliens take a bunch of people for meat, maybe some breeding pairs, and off they go, back to whatever shithole they came from. Then we take over."

"Why would they leave?" James again, in a monotone voice.

"Why the hell not?" Smelly Jay responded. "They came from somewhere, have a home."

"How do you know that?" James spoke again. Jay glared at him, then talked to the female member of their group.

"Sue. Take this one out and put a bullet in his brain. He just outlived his welcome."

"No!" Janice screamed and launched herself at the Boss. Surprised, Jay stumbled back as the no-name males started to laugh at the sight. The woman called Sue stepped forward, drawing a pistol as Jay fended off Janice.

Bob and Harry must have done a poor job of searching SSGT Sanchez. As they dragged her to the cabin, the commotion involving Janice caused them to turn and look. That was just the distraction the Sergeant needed. The Sergeant jerked her right arm free. As if by magic, a fighting blade appeared in her right hand. Bob screamed and sank to his knees as she stabbed and cut the knife into his groin. Sanchez then slashed the razor sharp blade across the knuckles of Harry's grasping hands, causing him to let go of the PJ. Camila Sanchez rolled onto her back and lashed out with her uninjured right leg into Harry's crotch. The man stumbled back, holding himself with his cut hands.

During the distraction, Matt grabbed his captors pistol and shoved it upward. It went off into the air as Matt drove his right knee into the no-name man's groin. Matt did a weapon rip his veteran father had taught him, breaking the trigger finger of the attacker. The Tribal Member then used the pistol to smash the no-name's face in, nose and all. The second no-name tried to unsling his rifle, finally spurred into action. Matt went to the ground and rolled, then shot the man between his eyes as the no-name finished unslinging his weapon.

The woman called Sue had her pistol but was momentarily confused as to who was her target. Then she was hit by James. Janice's brother did a perfect imitation of a football linebacker and knocked her flat. He then stomped on her face. The woman's pistol was in his hand as he turned and shot Smelly Jay in the face while the miscreant swung his baton at the screaming Janice. James then turned and shot both the no-name with the smashed face and Harry. James walked forward as if he were a machine, shifting to and fro with the pistol like a weapons turret on a fighting vehicle. James then walked up to bleeding Bob.

"James. *No!*" Janice screamed at her Brother. Sally was close enough and now stirred into action she was able to grab James around his waist. The combat spell was finally broken. James began to shake violently and plunked down. Janice was with him in a heartbeat.

"Hey, can I get some help?" SSGT Sanchez called out. "I'm bleeding like a stuck pig."

Matthew responded, kept the confiscated pistol close at hand. "Here. Use my emergency first aid pouch on my belt." Matt followed the PJs instruction and was soon using the bandages and other material in the pouch to stop the bleeding and bind the wound.

"Looks like a bullet went clean through, Ma'am."

"That's Sergeant. Ain't no officer, I work for a living." Sanchez watched as Matt expertly bandaged her thigh. "You have experience with gunshot wounds, young man?"

"Lots of hunting, so I know what a bullet can do. Plus some first aid classes my father and uncle made me take if I wanted to go hunting in the deep woods. They said there is no one to help you out there but yourself."

"Smart men." Sanchez used her chin to gesture over

Matts' shoulder.

"I think the a-hole known as Bob is bleeding out. Might want to help him."

"Why?" Asked Matt.

"Intel, my good man. Some answers."

"Okay." Matt rose and attended to Bob.

The man called Bob was white with shock and blood loss. Sergeant Sanchez' blade had cut deep and wide.

"Hey Janice," Matt called out. "Can you get that EMT bag you brought along?"

Janice untangled herself from James. He had finally stopped shaking but looked pale.

"I'll stay with him," Sally said. Janice nodded, stood up and went into the cabin.

"Hey people," Sanchez called out. "Can somebody go to what is left of the Blackhawk? Somewhere around there is my M-4."

James was suddenly awake in the world and called out. "I will."

"You sure?" Asked Sally. James smiled.

"I'm okay. The wire is reconnected." He stood up and strode to the wreckage.

Matt looked at the dying Bob.

"We'll help you, but we need to know what's going to happen next. Will aliens come? Will they? " He slapped Bob's face. "Answer me."

"They, they check in... with us... if we don't... call them." Bob's eyes began to flutter.

"Here's the bag, Matt," Janice said.

"Thanks. Now let's see about saving this..." The man called Bob shuddered, jerked, then lay still. Matt checked for a pulse and got none.

"Well so much for that idea," said Matt. He stood up and walked back to the Sergeant.

"Anyone else alive?" asked Sanchez.

"I will check," answered Matt.

"Where's James?" asked Janice.

"Went to check the Blackhawk for supplies, weapons," replied Sally.

"Damn," said Janice. Then she began to walk fast towards the wreckage.

Matt went to the woman called Sue and discovered James' head stomp had cracked her skull. Blood and fluid were oozing from what was left of her nose, mouth, and ears. Just as Matt knelt next to the woman, her body shuddered, and Matt heard what some people call the Death Rattle. She was dead. He stood up, and Sanchez called out.

"No Joy?"

"Wha... oh. No. She's dead. Bob said before he died, that the Aliens will check in with them periodically."

"Shit. Well," said the Sergeant, "we need transport out of here in skoshi time. I don't want to be here when any of their so-called friends show up." Sanchez muscled her way to standing, cursed from the pain as she tried to walk on her injured left leg. "I need a crutch."

"Here, I'll help," said Sally. Sanchez put her arm around her and hobbled to the cabin porch.

"You four, are you some kind of local trained group I don't know about? You people are mean and nasty, took care of these a-holes right quick."

"They did the heavy lifting, Sergeant," Sally replied. "I'm just seasonal help. Met them... day and a half ago? Can't say. No concept of time right now. It seems like... forever."

"Well, you four make a good team. Saved my bacon."

James and Janice returned at that moment. James had two assault rifles in his hands, and a tactical vest with rifle magazines slung over his shoulder. Janice had a Fritz helmet on her head and a matching tactical vest. She also had a bit of a pale face.

"I take it no one is alive?" asked Sergeant Sanchez. The

two Richards shook their heads 'no.'

"Well, it's just us," Sanchez paused for a couple of moments, then continued. "Who wants to go with me? I'm headed to a rallying point at Fairchild Air Force Base. We just need transport now." The four new friends all looked at each other, then all nodded 'yes' in unison. Sanchez laughed.

"You sure you all haven't worked together before?'

"Just my brother James and I," answered Janice.

"And we fight and argue," James added.

Sanchez laughed. "Well, if you don't mind. I'll be in charge," said the Sergeant. "If you do mind, find yourself another PJ."

"What's a PJ?" Asked Janice.

"Short for Pararescue," James interjected. "USAF Special Forces. Are trained in all the combat arts, are certified EMTs, scuba divers like the SEALS, Parachute and Airborne Qualified. They also have the highest washout rate of any special unit training.."

"Whoa, son! You trying out for a USAF recruiter's position?"

"He just... really remembers things, Sergeant," Janice said.

"Well, that is an excellent characteristic. Now, everyone on board? Good. Now, the transport time. Is that pickup workable?"

The new group of five were on the road in twenty minutes. Matt and James kicked out the ruined front windshield. It would be a windy ride until they could find a replacement, but the truck still drove. All their supplies were quickly loaded in the bed of the pickup, to include a dozen extra weapons, most taken from the dead renegade humans. Sanchez made the young people strip the six bodies of all usable items, including a couple of coats. They found just a few snacks so obtaining more food and water was a must. The Blackhawk had been pretty much burned out.

"Never thought I 'd be shot out of the sky in the U.S. with one of our Stinger Missiles," Camila Sanchez said.

"Sergeant," said Matt. "Sorry about all your buddies…"

"No good crying over spilled milk, like my *abuela* used to say in El Paso."

"Your grandmother?" Matt asked.

"Yep. She was a tough old woman. Passed on just last year." Camila Sanchez paused for a moment. Then continued.

"How old are you Matt?"

"Eighteen."

"The others?"

"James is seventeen I think, Janice sixteen. Sally... she never said."

"I'm twenty," Sally answered as she walked up.

"Okay, if I can get everyone's attention before I stretch out in the truck bed and rest my shot up left leg. You are all going to age real quick in the coming days and weeks. We are in a war." Camila let that concept sink in for a moment.

"From this day forward, you are all fighters. Because you are going to have to fight for survival against a truly alien enemy, who has traitors helping them. We have all lost, friends and family. We may lose more. But we cannot quit. Never. Unless you want to be eaten. For all the reports and suppositions are true. Each of us is meat on the hoof."

Every one of the five stood silent, lost in their own thoughts. Then James broke the silence. "Group Hug. For we are family."

Sergeant Sanchez tried to hide her tears as she knew she had to be tough right now. "Hell, why not? But we need a new family name also."

"Richards Raiders," James suggested.

They hugged each other then clambered into the pickup. Matt drove with James riding shotgun with one of the M-4 rifles. Matt's .44 Magnum Marlin was stashed behind the seat Everyone, even Sally, had a pistol stashed or holstered on their persons. The three women road in the truck bed with Sergeant Sanchez keeping an eye out with her M-4. They blocked out of their minds the bodies they left behind at the campground.

Matt turned onto Highway 2, taking it slow and smooth as the sun rose. With no windshield, they would be eating bugs galore if they drove too fast. Through the small town of Waterville, and then even smaller Douglas they drove. There were no humans to be seen.

"Intelligence reports said that the aliens are oceanic." said Camila. "They now own most of the coastal areas and areas around bodies of water."

"Why here?" asked Sally. "Lakes aren't that big."

"Columbia River. They can use it as a highway if they are really amphibious. The Spokane River isn't small either."

"Grand Coulee Dam? Would that be a barrier?" Janice asked.

"I doubt it. If it is, the aliens will just breach it with one of their weapons. Although they kept things like satellites intact, we think to use them later. They are not above using our power sources I think."

Matt called out through the driver's side window. "Gas gauge is dipping. I don't want to be stuck out in the middle of nowhere with no fuel."

"Good call, there is no Triple-A around anymore. Okay," instructed the Sergeant. "Keep an eye out for fuel sources. And food sources. I'm getting hungry."

"I still have some horse meat. A couple of pounds of it," informed Matt.

"Still count me out," said Janice. "We have some lunch meat and bread left."

"Well, Matt, the horse will do in a pinch. But let's see what else we can find."

"There should be a couple of MREs somewhere behind the driver's seat," added Sally.

"Ah, good ole MRE's," said Sanchez. "Well, at least they are better than the ole 'C' and 'K' Rations."

They were nearing Coulee City when James called out.

"Sergeant, what is that out in the field?" Camila Sanchez used the binoculars to scope out what James pointed out.

"Well, I'll be. A HUMVEE. Good eyes, James. Okay, Matt,

please pull over while we figure out how to do this."

"Don't you want to drive out to it?" asked Matt.

"Call me paranoid, but that could be bait for a nice Alien version of a mousetrap, with us being the mice." Sergeant Sanchez sat in the back of the truck and thought. Then, she slid herself to the end of the truck bed and slid out. She cursed as she tried to put weight on her injured leg. "Well, so much for that idea. Okay, Matt and James, I need you."

Janice frowned at the mention of James. "What do you need him for?"

"He and Matt are going out there and check that HUMVEE. If we are lucky, it will start."

"Ah, can I talk to you for a moment, Sergeant? In private?" asked Janice.

"We do not have time for that, sorry. A Delta can fly over at any minute, and we will be hiding in the tall grass. So please spit it out."

"Look. My brother has special needs," Janice said. "He is not like other people…"

"No, he is not like other people. He rose to the occasion instead of running and cowering. He took care of business with little training and a bunch of instinct. And. Most important to me, he saved *my* ass."

"And what will happen when he shorts out?" Janice shot back.

"Shorts out?" Camila was confused. "What?"

"She means when the loose wire in me flops the wrong way, and I freeze, or screw up. You could be hurt."

"Loose wire? You mean you may have a bit of a so-called mental condition and may not function correctly? Is that what you mean?"

"Yes. That is the way my Father explained it."

Sergeant Sanchez stood and stared at James and Janice for a few seconds. Then, she hobbled up to within inches of James' face. Camila was a bit stocky but was taller than many a

Mexican American. Thus, she did not have to look up much to see eye to eye with James. "You *will* remain focused. You *will not* flake out, short circuit, whatever. You will function and succeed just like you did at the campground. Am I clear?"

"Yes. Sergeant." James answered, his eyes a bit wide.

"I can't hear you!"

"Yes, Sergeant!"

"Good. Now you and Matt will take your weapons and check out the HUMVEE. If you see a threat, you will engage it, while I provide cover fire from Back here. Got it?"

"Yes, Sergeant!"

Camila looked at Matt.

"I got it the first time, Sergeant," said Matt.

Within minutes the two males, after a crash course in mutual support, was walking out towards the HUMVEE. Janice had a bit of a pout on as she used a twenty-two rifle to help cover her brother. Sanchez had the other M-4 with the A-COG sight system scanning the area around the HUMVEE. Sally was up in the truck cab, ready to haul ass out if they were attacked.

"You can glare at me all you want, Missy, but it won't change things," Camila Sanchez said without taking her eyes off the two males.

"You don't understand," protested Janice.

"Yes, I do. Because I could have been James in my family."

"What?"

"I was different. I didn't act like the little *chica* my family wanted me to be. They accused me of being a lesbian, a slut, an asshole, threatened to send me to a convent to straighten me out." Sanchez paused a moment as she checked out a flock of birds disturbed by the two young men. "So I ran away. I got some phony documents, and enlisted in the U.S. Air Force."

Sanchez looked at Janice as she continued. "I was sixteen. As soon as I could, I started applying to the most demanding careers I could. I was one of the first women to make it through the PJs training. Now I am an old woman at age twenty-five. I was supposed to tack on my fifth stripe next week. Then this." Sanchez scanned the area around the HUMVEE again. "Given the chance, people often rise to the occasion. If you coddle them, protect them. Sit on them because you are afraid they will fail, and they will never rise. They may become moles instead, hiding in the dirt." Sanchez looked at Janice. "You think James is a mole?"

"Of course I don't!" Janice replied.

"Then don't keep trying to bury him in low expectations."

Ten minutes later, two young men grinning like idiots had the HUMVEE parked next to the pickup. Sergeant Sanchez hobbled over to the vehicle and began trying to crawl around in it as much as she could with a shot up left leg. She soon sang out.

"Hot damn! A Stinger Missile in its case. Some forty mike-mike grenades with a launcher we can hook on to something, like an M-4. A flare gun and flares. An old M-9 pistol with a box of nine-millimeter ammo. *And* some munchies. We are in hog heaven, troops!" Somehow, she extracted herself from the vehicle, as Matt and James stood next to it.

"We did well?" Matt asked.

"You are *muy excellente!*" Sanchez said with a large grin on her face. She glanced over at Janice. "You rose to the expectations we needed. Now, let's get the stuff transferred and mount up."

The fact the HUMVEE had a full tank of fuel and a large jerrycan of fuel was a godsend. When asked, Sergeant Sanchez had no idea what happened to the original crew.

"They might have panicked, bugged out for some reason," she said. "There was no blood, so I guess no one harvested them. At least not nearby."

Sergeant Sanchez had one of the group standing and

watching through the top hatch of the HUMVEE, specifically for the Deltas and the 'Falcon' discs. Surprisingly, no action of any kind was seen. They made good time with Matt still driving. Coulee City was a ghost town, with a couple of burning buildings exhibiting the lack of response by anyone. The group kept moving and passed through other small towns with much the same result. Even a somewhat larger town of Davenport seemed deserted.

"Where is everyone?" asked Sally Card.

"I believe it is the War of the Worlds effect, but this time for real," responded James.

"You mean that radio broadcast in the 1940's that scared everyone?"

"Yes. This time though, there are Aliens in the skies. They may all be heading East as West means being attacked and may be eaten."

"Well," added the Sergeant, "it makes sense. EBS started with shelter in place then changed to run like hell."

"The military heard that?" asked Janice from her lookout point in the overhead hatch.

"I guess its time for the whole story," said Sanchez. "For the first twelve hours, it was all a 'natural disaster of biblical proportions.' We were suckered into thinking the rocks were from an unnoticed meteor shower. Then, the Harvester Arks, Delta fighters, and those great saucer things someone started calling Falcons because they look straight out of a movie set."

The Sergeant took a drink from a water bottle before she continued. "McChord Air Field had taken a direct from a trailer size rock. Which wiped out the runways and a lot of the air assets. The Deltas then came in, strafing anything that moved. When they showed up, we really knew it was an Invasion."

"The president?" Asked James.

"Dead as far as we know. Along with the Vice. We were told before we launched in our Blackhawk that one of the Space Arks was sitting on the front lawn of the White House. All communications with D.C. are gone."

"Who made the decision that everyone head inland?" Matt asked from the driver's seat.

"The Acting President. The former Secretary of Veterans Affairs. Yes, most of Congress, the Courts, and the Executive Branch in Washington D.C. are either dead or in hiding. So, we launched to do recon for a bunch of military vehicles stuffed to the gills with Active Duty and Civilians. You saw the rest. Goddamn traitors."

"Think any of those people in vehicles will make it?" Sally asked.

"I can hope, Sally. I can hope. I lost eight friends on the 'Hawk. I don't want it to be in vain."

"Well, Sergeant, now you have more friends," James stated.

"That I do, boyo. That I do."

An hour later of careful driving, they were in the outskirts of Spokane. They hit the remains of Fairchild Air Force Base on the West Side of the city. It was a mass of fiery black plumes of smoke. Sergeant Sanchez tried to keep it together but failed. She began to scream and rage, tears streaming down her face.

"You alien fuckers! Sneak up, throw rocks at us, then blow us up. What did we ever do to you? Huh? *What did we do?!*" Camila Sanchez pounded the ceiling of the HUMVEE in rage. James put his hand on her arm.

"You'll help us make it. Sergeant. It won't be in vain."

"Oh yeah? Well, that still doesn't answer 'why.' Why Earth? Why us?"

"Because... we taste good," James stated. Everyone's mouth in the HUMVEE dropped open at James rather blunt comment. Then, Sergeant Sanchez burst out laughing. The tough PJ hugged the young man.

"My man, you have a way about you," the Sergeant said. She unclasped from him and wiped her eyes.

"You know what? I plan on making us the most unappetizing item on the menu," the PJ stated. "If they eat me, I'll make sure they get sicker than a dog with worms. Now, let me see those maps we scrounged. Matt, take it slow. James. Shotgun seat with the M-4. I doubt if there is much government control around."

Matt wove the HUMVEE slowly through Airway Heights and into Spokane, Washington. He went down a highway offramp and onto a city street. Unlike previous population centers, there were a lot of people milling around. Many of the residents and passers-through seemed in shock. And of course, there were those who appeared to be taking advantage of the weak and confused.

"Do we stop, Sergeant?" asked Matt.

"Not downtown. I think law and order are gone." Sanchez shifted the map around. "There are nuke bases in Montana and North Dakota They will have hardened facilities and survivors, I bet you. Then, we can plan on payback to these Squids."

"Squids?" asked Janice.

"Oh. I forgot that detail. Navy types say the creatures that seem to be in control are these big, whatchacallit, cephalo...."

"Cephalopods. Squids, cuttlefish, and octopi," James informed the others. "Very intelligent—even the native ones on Earth."

"Yeah. Well this PJ has a new hankering for calamari and sushi... the outer space kind."

The companions began to laugh. Then Matt braked the HUMVEE. "Sergeant. Military people," Matt said. A man in a set of combat fatigues was standing in the middle of the road with his hand out in a 'stop' gesture.

"Help me get out, would ya Sally?" said Sanchez. "Matt, James, cover me from behind the vehicle doors. These have

Kevlar plates in them. Janice, keep an eye out up in the hatch." Sergeant Sanchez managed to hobble to the front of the HUMVEE, leaned against the right fender. The figure approaching seemed to have Lieutenants bars on his collars. But his hair was too long, and he had old style black combat boots on, not the current brushed leather.

"Sergeant, report please," the Lieutenant stated. Camila did her best to stand straight with her injured leg and saluted.

"Sir, Staff Sergeant Sanchez. USAF Pararescue, late of McChord Air Force Base."

"I see you have saved a HUMVEE, very good, Sergeant." The officer had a military issued gun belt on with a new looking M-17 pistol. But, he just did not seem right to Sanchez.

"I'll have to commandeer the vehicle, Sergeant. Sorry. Military necessity." The officer gestured over his shoulder, and three scruffy looking individuals walked out from behind some parked vehicles. They held non-standard military-style rifles, the barrels at least pointed at the ground.

"Ah. Sir. Not to be disrespectful, but do you have some orders, or ID or something else…"

"Sergeant, you are disobeying a superior officer. You realize the ramifications of that action?" The man tried to sound gruff and commanding.

"Sir, with all due resp—" Sanchez never finished the sentence. Rounds from behind her zipped by her right ear. The PJ instinctively ducked, then went to the pavement as she tried to draw a pistol. It took her a moment to realize that James had opened up with his M-4 Assault Rifle. Bullets slammed into the three approaching figures before they could react and they all went down. Sanchez twisted on the ground and looked up at Matt. He had the Beretta he had taken from the dead horse days ago screwed in the fake lieutenants ear.

James kept advancing and shooting until his magazine was empty. He did this even after the armed men were down and bled. Sanchez managed to lever her self back to standing using the bumper and hood of the vehicle. James kept trying to fire the empty M-4 like some automaton at an old amusement park. Finally, Janice grabbed him and dragged him back to the HUMVEE. Sergeant Sanchez began to curse loud and fluently in Spanish as Matt relieved the alleged officer of his pistol.

"Hands on your head, asswipe," Camila told the man with the officer's rank insignia. Matt stepped back as the man complied.

"Hey, Sergeant. We were just—"

"*Shut up!*" Camila screamed at the man. Somehow she stumbled over and whipped her pistol across the fake officers face. He stumbled and fell.

"What is your name. Your *name.*"

"Fred Sanders." His lips were bloody from the impact of the pistol.

"Well, Fred. You just got you three friends killed because you wanted a ride out of here. Matt, I'll cover him. You take the magazines out of those rifles, unload the chambers, and heave the rifles in that trash can over there. We'll keep the magazines. Then tie ass wipe up."

"Look it," Sanders started to say. Camila pointed her pistol at his face.

"One more word and you eat a bullet."

There were no more words.

II

Ten minutes later, Sanders was tied up, and the three bodies drug to the side of the street. Camila had Matt tied up the fake officer a bit loose so he could eventually get free. Camila did not think Sanders would be a threat without his toadies. She did not question him further, did not care why he tried to take the HUMVEE and got his buddies killed. Camila Sanchez, Staff Sergeant, had a more pressing problem. James Richards.

She hobbled to the back of the HUMVEE where Janice had James sequestered. The sister was trying to soothe her brother as Camila worked her way to them.

"James, why did you do that? Why did you shoot them? That's not like you."

"Yeah, James, why did you shoot them," the Sergeant repeated the question.

"They were going to hurt us," answered James.

"How could you tell? Huh? How could you?" questioned Camila.

"You leave him alone, Sanchez," Janice spat at her. "You're the one who got him in this mess. I told you he was different, had problems."

"That still does not answer the question. What did you see that the rest of us did not?"

"I just saw and analyzed," James answered.

"Analyzed what?" demanded Camila

"Them. It. The situation. I can't explain it. I just see stuff. Feel and know stuff."

Sergeant Sanchez paused for a moment as she looked at James. The young man's instincts were probably correct. But the way he kept acting, blasting away at men already down and dying, was the problem.

"Okay. Get this through your skull, troop. You do that again, off people after they are down and out, and I will put you down like the mad dog you would become."

"You can't—" Janice started to say, but Camila interrupted.

"Lady, I will not save a psychopath. If you want to stay with him, great. Take your stuff and walk. But if you two stay with me... the statement stands." The Sergeant managed to stand in front of James and bored through him with her eyes.

"You understand, James? Summary: execution if you do that shit again."

Before Janice could intercede, James said, "Yes, Sergeant."

"Good," replied Camila. "Mount up."

Camila had Matt get back on Interstate 90 headed East. She wanted out of Spokane, refueled or not. The group crossed into Idaho, and a few miles outside of Coeur d'Alene, they came across a ditched tanker truck. A quick check found it was full of diesel, fuel the engine of the HUMVEE could handle. It took them about an hour, but the finally managed to refuel the vehicle by filling whatever additional container they had and poured it into the HUMVEE, The refilled the jerrycan they had as well as a couple of whiskey bottles they found in the semi-truck cab. Again, no sign of where the driver had gone.

"Somebody must be grabbing people," Matt said.

"That is a scary thought," said Camila.

"But it is the explanation," replied Matt. "No Deltas are blasting. No Falcon battlecruisers are picking up the freshly killed humans. No sight of a Harvester Ark as the Military named them. So, where is everyone? They can't all be hiding."

"Well, there is a Greyhound Park and Event Center ahead," said Camila. "With all this stress, my injury, we need some rest. The word we had was that the so-called Squids are staying near the Coast or large bodies of water. So, we stop and rest. I doubt if anyone is racing dogs today."

The group made camp at the back end of a large parking area. There were a couple of abandoned cars in the lot but again, no sign of people.

"They were scared off," said James.

"How do you know that?" Camila asked.

"I just know it," James replied. Again, a funny instinct no one else had.

"Well, James, keep your weapon near you. But no shooting just because you feel like it. Got it?"

"Yes. Sergeant."

Matt and James went down to the Spokane River which was only a quarter mile away for some water and to see any sign of fish or small game. Sally and Janice went to check out the two abandoned cars and see if any of the Dog Park was open. Thus, Camila sat and rested her injured leg while she guarded the HUMVEE. It was actually lovely to be alone with her own thoughts for a while. Then Janice and Sally returned with some booty.

"Some chips, apples and baking potatoes, with some condiment packets. If you start a fire, we can roast the potatoes," said Sally.

"Sounds good to me. Grab some free wood, shrubs, No one is around to complain about a campfire with no camp."

Matt and James returned with a couple of grasshoppers James had caught. "You can eat these, right, Sergeant?" James inquired.

"Yes James, you can. But let's roast and eat the potatoes first. Plus, you still have a little of that horsemeat left, Matt?"

"Yep, sure do."

"Well, we have the makings of a meal. Maybe an MRE also to add to the variety."

The five survivors were soon cooking the first substantial meal in days. Everyone roasted potato on a stick, plus the rest to the horsemeat. Even Janice ate some of the meat. They split up an MRE Chili pack, then passed out the apples. The small group was soon satiated.

"I'm going to take a small walk, look for a restroom," said Matt.

"Can I join you on the walk, Matt?" Janice asked.

"Sure."

"Take your weapons," Camila said.

"Yes, Sergeant," Janice replied with less than friendly tone.

The two young people were soon walking up towards the main buildings of the Greyhound Park.

"I think Sally and I saw some bathroom signs over there,"

"Okay. I have a flashlight, so that should help. The Sun's beginning to set."

They found the facilities and shared the flashlight, they soon found the water system still worked, so they felt halfway normal. As they slowly walked back to the HUMVEE, they talked.

"What do you think of the Sergeant?" asked Janice

"She's tough. Has to be," replied Matt.

"She's too tough," said Janice. "She thinks everyone can

be as tough as she is. Well, James isn't."

"You know, Janice, I know you love your brother and want to protect him But say something happens to you? Then what?"

"Don't say that, Matt." Replied Janice.

"But you have to accept it. Not to be mean, but, well... we both lost our families."

Janice was silent for a minute as they walked, then she stopped and turned towards Matt. "Make me a promise, Matt."

"What, Janice?"

"If something happens to me, you'll watch out for James."

"Of course. We're friends."

"No, I really mean this," pushed Janice. "Take care of like family. Like a brother. Please?"

Matt looked into Janice's eyes and even in the reduced light of the setting sun, saw they were a pretty deep blue. Funny how he had not noticed that before. "Okay, Janice. Deal. Shake." Matt stuck his hand out and Janice closed the distance and kissed him instead. One kiss led to another, and soon they were in a deep embrace. Finally, they separated.

"Janice..."

"Shhhh. Don't say anything. This is between us. Okay?"

"Okay. But this whole situation... "

"Is not right for a relationship," Janice said. "But let's just see what happens. We have to live life still." Matt signed, then kissed her on the lips one last time.

"Okay. Now, we need to get back, before the Sergeant sends out a search party."

Camila was doing a weapons check of the firearms they collected over the previous days. As she did, she wrote it down in a small notebook she always carried and talked a bit to herself.

"Two M-4s, a civilian AR-15, two twelve gauge pumps, a

twenty-two semi-auto rifle, an SKS and an old bolt action Mauser rifle. Add to that a total of seven handguns since we seized that one from idiot Fred, we have a small arsenal. Oh, plus Matts lever action Magnum. Sufficient ammunition for the M-4s and AR-15, some ammo for the rest. Doing good for Richard's Raiders."

Camila looked up as Matt and Janice walked up. She suppressed a smile as she got the vibes that maybe something nice was forming between the two.

"Anything interesting?" asked Camila.

"Water system still works," Matt replied.

"Hmmm. Maybe we can have some quick makeshift baths in the morning. Then on to Montana."

"Why Montana?"

"Malmstrom Air Force Base—it's a nuke base, so it has hardened facilities, especially in the ICBM Fields spread out around the city. Thus, I bet lots of survivors as I have not heard of any nukes being used by the Squids as we call them. Cheyenne Moutain may have been taken out by a nuke. That is the only one I know of in the U.S."

"Why didn't the Squids use atomic weapons?" Matt asked.

"Didn't have to," answered Camila. "Kinetic energy developed by those rocks they threw at us acted like small nukes when big enough. And no radiation to spoil the meat."

"This is sick," Janice said. "Being hunted by some Bug-Eyed Monsters, BEMs, who know we are intelligent yet look at us as food."

"Ants look and act intelligent," James said as he walked up and joined the conversation. "Maybe these Squids as you call them just think we are social creatures like ants."

"Could be, James. But that is above my pay grade." Answered Camila. "Now, I suggest we get out scrounged bedding together and get some rest. I'll take the first watch, wake up the next person. Then down the line. We all pull watch duty."

"Could I have a private conversation with you, Sergeant?" Janice asked.

"Okay. Let me hobble over to that bench someone was so nice to put in a parking lot."

Sally had found a substantial branch which Camila could use as a cane and move with a bullet-holed leg. The two women sat down facing each other.

"Look, Sergeant," began Janice. "I know we are in a bad situation. But I don't want James to be turned into a psycho killer. So, how about limit what he has to do?" Camila paused for a moment before answering. She had to remember she was dealing with very young civilians, not trained soldiers or airmen. Camila also realized her abilities at age sixteen may have been more significant than the three eighteen years and younger persons who were now attached to her at the hip.

"Okay, Janice. I get your point. But I have little control over what we may face until we get to some installation where there will be aid and a bit more security. So, we do what we must. I may have been a bit harsh about the shooting comment. However, I can neither allow any dead weight to endanger the rest of you, nor an out of control individual."

"You hit it on the head, Sergeant. Harsh is the word," responded Janice. "If we lose our humanity, how will we then compare to these... *Squids* who see us as meat?"

Camila sighed. Janice had a point. The Sergeant was trying to pull off a delicate balancing act between survival and maintaining some resemblance of human caring.

"Okay. Point taken, Janice. So, please help me keep James as a productive member of our group. Please."

"Agreed. Shake." Said Janice. The two women may never actually agree, but they could at least work together.

Janice and Camila made their way back to the HUMVEE,

where the Sergeant took half a pain pill form their medical supplies. Her left leg was throbbing.

"You okay?" Sally asked.

"As well as can be expected with a leg with a bullet hole that I can't stay off. And, I don't want to be fuzzy due to pain meds."

"Well, Sergeant, let me know if I can help," said Sally.

"Call me Camila. I keep forgetting you all are civilians, not trained troops."

Sally smiled. "Okay, Camila. Deal."

The five survivors had their beds made as the Sun set behind the mountains. No street lights nor building lights came on, signifying the local power grid was down.

"Okay. I have the first watch," Camila said. "I'll wake the next volunteer."

"That'll be me," said Sally. "I need to pull my weight."

"You got it."

The four companions were soon asleep in various sleeping bags and bedrolls. Camila kept the fire at a low ebb as she tried to see around her. It was odd to be in almost complete blackness while sitting next to a major city. The Sergeant had of course been in combat areas with little or no power. However, she never imagined experiencing this in the United States. At least the sky was clear, and the Moon and stars provided some light. Camila sat back on a scrounged patio chair James had found.

"Better than a sharp stick in the eye," she mused to herself.

Four hours later, Camila woke Sally up.

"Why didn't you get me up earlier?" scolded the Forest Service employee.

"I'm an old hand at this. You are not," replied Camila. "You needed the sleep."

"Okay. Well, my turn. Go to bed. That's an order."

"Yes. Ma'am," Camila added with a chuckle.

The Sergeant was soon asleep as Sally managed to heat up some water for instant coffee. "Oof," Sally said as she took a sip of the black drink. "Definitely not Starbucks."

As she sipped her coffee, she thought she heard something. Sally stood up from the patio chair and cocked her head to listen. There it was again. A dog whining.

"Here pup," Sally whispered as she made her way towards the sound. She had a pistol in her hand. Sally knew how to shoot but was never into actually shooting at something or someone. Thus, she never had any desire for a Law Enforcement Ranger position in the Forest Service. Helping people and other living things were more her style.

"Here pup," she whispered again. And there it was. Clearly, a greyhound let loose from the dog track. Sally had read that they were gentle creatures who loved humans and to run. So, Sally was hoping the dogs love for humans would outweigh its desire to run.

"Come on, pup. Come to Sally. Oh, you have a rope on you. Are you caught?" Sally moved closer as she whispered.

Something strong, long, but with a live flesh feeling wrapped itself around Sally. The grasping member had aimed for her neck but due to her being bent over and in the dark caused the rope-like appendage to miss its mark. Sally could scream... and scream she did, as she shot at the bulk arising from the darkness.

amila tried to bound up from her rack and almost fell over due to her forgotten injured led. Matt made it up from his bedroll in a flash, ran towards Sally's screams with his .44 Magnum. James and Janice were up, holding weapons, both confused.

"Stay here," ordered the Sergeant as she tried to hobble after Matt. The Marlin Magnum rifle spoke with a loud report as Camila cursed.

Matt made it to where Sally was entangled with something. He fired at a second figure coming up from the Spokane Riverbed, then spun for a shot at whatever had Sally. Something long and snakelike whipped at Matt's head, and he blocked it with his rifle. Sally screamed, and a shot rang out from her pistol. There were a smashing sound and something rolled against Matt's feet. As Matt backpedaled away from whatever was trying to grab him, he saw the object on the ground. It was Sally's head. He screamed.

An M-4 opened up on the two dark bulks near the

humans. Camila fired all but a couple of rounds from her magazine as she switched from one target to the other. Her rifle's attached flashlight illuminated the results of the gunfire. Two clearly cephalopod creatures lay bleeding a bluish substance that must be their version of human blood. Their many arms twitched for a few moments, then they were still. One large grasping tentacle still held a staff weapon with a sickle-shaped blade at the end. There was splashed human blood around where the weapon lay. Matt stepped up next to Camila and vomited. The Sergeant slapped his arm.

"Be sick later. Make sure those two things are dead." Matt nodded, then went to the task. Camila glanced at Sally's decapitated head. At least, she thought, Sally had died a relatively quick death. Better than waiting on the butcher's block.

"These pieces of shit used this greyhound as bait," Matt said as he walked up with a whining greyhound dog with its mouth taped shut. "Taped its mouth shut so it couldn't bark or bite. Hobbled its legs also."

"They know us," said Camila. "They know us too well. Sally ventilated that one there even as it... killed her. At least we know they die as we do."

James and Janice walked up at that moment.

"What happened?" asked Janice. She screamed when she saw the human and alien corpses. Matt pushed the greyhound at James, grabbed Janice and led her away. James stood with the dog's rope leash in his hand, staring at the bodies. Camila realized he was not just staring but examining. Before the Sergeant could say anything, he starting speaking.

"That weapon looks old. See what looks like writing on it? I think these two... Squids were trying to hunt in some traditional way. Much like some Native American tribes on the West Coast demand, they are allowed to hunt whales as that is their tradition. Matt hunts on ancient tribal land because that is what his ancestors did. This is not harvesting. This was hunting."

Camila looked at James. Damn, he did observe and analyze better than most people. If that was a side effect of his 'condition' his loose wire, it might help fight off the Squids.

"You have a camera, James?" She asked.

"I still have some charge on my cell phone," answered James. "I think I can film using it."

"Good," said Camila. "I'll take the dog, and get something to wrap Sally up with. I'm not going to leave her here for some Squid to snack on. Film as much as you can, and grab that alien weapon. Intelligence people will want to see it. Keep your M-4 handy."

James nodded and set to work.

Camila slowly made her way back to the HUMVEE with the greyhound. The dog had attached himself to the humans as dogs and humans have done for eons. The Sergeant became angry when she thought of the Squids using man's best friend to catch and eat humans. As she neared the HUMVEE, she saw Janice shaking as Matt held on to her. Seeing a new friend dead, decapitated, was not easy for anyone. The greyhound, sensing a human who was sad, moved towards Janice, tail wagging. He snuffled her and Janice along with Matt scratched the dog's ears.

"Hey, I need some help with a piece of tarp we have, I need it for... Sally."

"Okay, sure," answered Janice, as Matt nodded 'yes.' Within a few minutes, the three humans were down by the river and picked up Sally's remains. The greyhound followed them, and when the dog caught the scent of the dead Squids, he began barking, growing and snapping. Camila watched with interest.

"I think these aliens have a natural enemy. Our canine friends hate them."

"They will make good early warning systems," interjected James.

The four people placed the remains of their friend in the

piece of tarp. Camila wrapped the head up in a portion of the large plastic bag and put it with the body. Each of the four took a corner of the burden as if they were part of an official burial detail. They secured the body to the hood of the HUMVEE and broke camp. No one felt like sleeping there ever again.

They drove down until they found a small campground on the edge of the Coeur d' Alene National Forest. The location seemed fitting for a former Forest Service Employee. They used some entrenching tools along with some scrounged shovels to dig a grave. They laid Sally Card to rest.

"Can I say a few words?" asked James.

"Of course you can," said Camila. Janice took his hand as he spoke.

"We knew you only a short time. But you became family. We love you, Sally Card, and always will. Rest in peace until we meet again."

Camila quickly wiped her tears. She had to be strong for these civilians.

"I'll save these map coordinates. Someone will build a monument here if I have to do it myself."

"Good reason to stay in touch," said Matt.

"Yes, it is," said Camila. The greyhound walked over and laid next to the grave. The humans were afraid he would stay there, but when Camila said "Here, boy. We need you," the canine seemed to know just how true that was. As the four humans and a best friend settled in the HUMVEE, Janice spoke up.

"Hey, our new friend here needs a name, He had no collar and probably just had a racing number at the Dog Park."

"Flash," said, James.

"Why Flash?" Asked Matt.

"Well, the dog is fast, and the Flash is a comic super hero. I always liked him."

"Hey, Flash. You like that name?" asked Camila. Flash

wagged his tail as he licked her face.

The four plus one traveled down Interstate 90 and soon passed into Montana. The highway had been almost deserted, the group seeing or moving by only some dozen occupied vehicles since burying Sally Card. Sunrise had been about an hour prior when they thought they saw a flash of light from the Southwest. Then a deep rumbling noise shook the HUMVEE and the area around it. Matt pulled over to the side of the freeway.

"What the hell was that?" Mat asked.

"Let me look," said Camila. They helped her up through the roof hatch, and the Sergeant looked towards the Southwest with the binoculars.

"Oh shit."

"What's up, Sergeant Sanchez?" asked Janice. Camila sat back down in the HUMVEE. "Drive. Now. Someone set off a nuke down by the Tri-Cities area."

"Hanford is down in that direction," said James.

"If what you are suggesting just happened, James, we need to drive real fast. There is a mushroom-shaped fallout cloud rising over Eastern Washington as we speak. Winds will blow it East, just like the winds blew Mount Saint Helens ash east."

"So the Hanford Nuclear Site blew?" asked Janice.

"Could be," answered James. "The Squids may have set it off. Even by accident."

"Please drive faster, Matt," directed Camila. "The bigger the explosion, the higher the crap in the cloud climbs, the more chance it gets blown on us."

Matt soon had the HUMVEE zipping down Interstate 90 at some seventy miles an hour.

"There are some high mountain peaks between Eastern Washington and us," said James. "They should provide some protective barrier."

"Are they sixty thousand feet high?" asked Camila.

"Why? No."

"Drive fast, Matt. Then if we find a highway tunnel, we camp out for a while." Matt's speed soon ate up the miles. A high altitude vast cloud seemed to be growing in a northeasterly direction, which meant any fallout may stretch into at least West Montana. As they traveled down Interstate 90, more and more vehicles suddenly appeared and joined them, Going on five days since the Invasion and finally people were panicking and fleeing away from the coastal states.

"Wished I knew what the Military was doing," said Camila.

"No SATPHONE, or long-range radio?" asked Janice.

"Lost all that when the Stinger took the Blackhawk out. Hey, try the HUMVEE radio. Its shorter in range, but after I saw Fairchild blown to hell, I thought everything was toast."

"You'll have to try it, Sergeant. I have no idea how to operate this thing. I'm just the driver."

Camila managed to slide into the shotgun seat, swapping out with James. That resulted in many choice curse words as the Sergeants injured leg began to throb.

"Don't get shot, people. It hurts days later." It took a few minutes, but Camila finally got the radio set working. At least, the power indicator light came on. She tried various frequencies and call signs. Nothing.

"You have the Ham Radio Freqs on that thing?"

"I think. Let me try..."

Right around 479 Kilohertz, just below the commercial AM band, they picked some broadcasting.

"Military emergency transmission, who is this?" Camila broadcast.

"What? Is someone listening? I thought everyone was dead!"

"You're not a normal Ham Radio operator, are you? Over."

"No. Ma'am. Just call me Sam. I'm hiding out in a cabin

near Marshal Mountain, by Missoula, Montana. I managed to get this thing turned on, and just started talking."

"Sam, why are you up there? And why isn't anyone broadcasting anymore? Over."

"My friend Tim, the real Ham Operator, said the space aliens started homing in on radio transmissions to find military targets. That and a lot of crap was thrown up into the atmosphere when the rocks hit. So, not much talking. And some of those Arks are flitting around, landing near cities to grab people. Then they take off. I guess everyone is hiding."

" Any word on Malmstrom Air Force Base? Over."

"Nope. The EBS said a day ago to bug out from the Coast, go inland. I'm waiting for…"

Static. Then Silence. Camila swore.

"Well, Hanford blowing up won't help the communication systems around here either. We're still on our own."

"Still keep hauling ass?" Matt asked.

"Yep. We coming up on Missoula?"

"Yes, Sergeant."

"Well, we'll see how things are there, That will help us chose our route to Great Falls and Malmstrom Air Force Base."

Missoula, Montana was a madhouse. It looked as if every panicked person finally took the Bug Out Broadcast to heart. Matt wove his way through many a stalled vehicle or frightened group of people on Interstate 90. The fact they were driving a military vehicle and Camila had her Fritz helmet on gave people pause before they approached. Even to the panicked, the military seemed to mean something.

As they came upon the main exits into Downtown Missoula, they finally saw a couple of local police cars at the side of the Interstate. They seemed to be using their mere presence to keep people in some form of order. One of them saw the HUMVEE and waved them over. Camila leaned out the shotgun seat window.

"You officers are not having a good time, are you?" A tall and broad black male officer stepped up to the HUMVEE, laughing.

"Understatement of the year, Sergeant. Officer Power here and my pale friend over that is Officer Rogers, late of the Missoula Police Department."

"Late of, as in the Department no longer exists?"

"The City Council bugged out to the ski and resort areas to hide. All other First Responders were running around chasing meteor reports and fires. Then some of those damned Delta fighter types showed up and started shooting up all the tall buildings, and any fuel storage tanks they saw. Nothing like a full-fledged panic."

"So what Officer Power is saying," interjected Officer Rogers, "is that we have no real command structure, so thus no police department. Reports of Hanford in Washington going up in smoke doesn't help."

"You two veterans?" Camila asked.

"I'm Army," said Powers. "He's a Former Marine."

"Oorah," Rogers responded.

"Sergeant, are you part of the big wave of the military we were told are headed this way?" asked Powers.

"Well. To be honest," replied Camila. "I was the Recon Unit, the tip of the spear so to speak. Now, I have no idea where the shaft is. Other than the shaft the Squids are giving us."

"They really Squids, Sergeant?" Rogers asked.

"I have some pictures on my cell phone," James interjected. Camila glared at him, then turned back to the two Officers.

"Trust me. We need to save that phone use for our Intelligence folks. But if you see anything the size of s black bear with too many arms and legs, shoot it. They will try to eat you."

The two police officers exchanged glances. Then Rogers asked, "Where are you headed?"

"Malmstrom Air Force Base. If it still exists. Fairchild is toast."

"Well, that is where we are supposed to tell you to go," said Powers. "But turn off up here onto State Road 200. Follow it and the train tracks to Malmstrom. It's the shortest route, and you won't be such a target."

"Targets?" asked Matt.

"Target, as in Deltas and escapees from the State Prisons. Somebody or something targeted those places and busted the walls down. It has a plan on how to screw us."

Camila cursed long and hard. "They know us too well. The Squids know how to push out buttons, made some of us turn traitor." Camila stuck her hand out the window to shake hands with the two Cops.

"If anyone asks, Sergeant Camila Sanchez was here, headed to Malmstrom."

"Will do, Sergeant. You stay safe out there," stated Rogers.

Matt moved the HUMVEE back into traffic. People stayed out of their way once again. They found the sign for State Road 200 and managed to turn off. It was a lot less crowded as most people had this desire to clump up on the Interstate. As if there was safety in numbers.

"They're like lemmings," said Matt. "They follow the crowd to God knows what."

"You know, Walt Disney faked that movie footage," James said.

"Of the lemmings?" asked Matt.

"Yes. The producers chased a group of them and then threw them off the cliff to get the shots for the film."

"James," said Camila. "TMI. Too much information."

The road was windy but in good condition. Matt drove slower as he watched the gas gauge.

"We'll need to put that ten gallons in pretty soon,

Sergeant."

"Okay, Matt. Look for a small local Stop and Rob with fuel pumps. That may help also."

At the small town of Dvando, with the gas gauge on E, they found a little combination of country store and restaurant. It had power, so the group figured they should be able to pump some gas.

"I think we need a hot meal. And there are no bodies of water for Squids to hide in."

"What about Flash?" asked James.

"Go to the store, get some dog food for him, and a dog dish. I think he's going to be with us for a while."

"Ah, money? I have five dollars," said James.

"Here. I still have most of my prom money."

Camila looked at Janice, confused, after she spoke

"What? You never had prom money, Sergeant?"

"I never had a prom. And you can call me Camila. Sacrificing for a stray dog tells me that under that gruff exterior beats the heart of a softy."

"Right back at cha!" Janice said with a smile.

James went in the store part with Flash, and the rest went into the restaurant. An older woman was talking to one about Matt's age when the three walked in. The older woman called out, "Sit anywhere. As you can tell all this crap going on has killed business."

"I'm surprised you're open," said Matt. The older woman with the look of having worked in many a diner shrugged.

"What else are we going to do? Let the food rot while we sit at home?"

The young raven-haired waitress giggled and smoothed her dress as she walked up to Matt. "Hi. I'm Eve," she said as she flashed he best come-hither smile. Janice suddenly grabbed Matt's hand.

"Come on dear, let's sit at this table in the back."

Camila tried not to laugh at this new show of possessiveness. She thought she saw something the other night before Sally… the Sergeant buried that memory.

As they sat down with the now disappointed waitress off to get waters and menus, Matt looked at Camila. He must have noticed something in her previous look.

"So, you ever been married?" Matt asked.

"To a person, no. To my fellow PJs, yes."

"No one special?" asked Janice as she kept hold of Matt's hand.

"Yeah. A couple of times. But, well, I still have a slight confusion."

The two young people looked at each other. "You're, what. Gay? Lesbian?" Janice asked.

Camila laughed. "No. But what I am is one of those people who seems to like both genders, sexes. I tried to explain to a woman once who said she was a lesbian that I was bisexual and she got all pissed, said if I had sex with a woman, I was lesbian. I said if I had sex with a man also, what was I, she said a confused lesbian. So I guess I'm confused." Janice and Matt both laughed.

"After all this…" Camila waved her hand through the air. "I don't know what will happen. Right now, I just want to stay alive. And get your people to safety."

"You know, you don't have to do that. Get us to safety," said Matt.

"Yeah, I do," the Sergeant answered.

"Why? We were strangers a day or so ago."

"Let me ask you then, Matt. Why did you hook up and stay with James and Janice? Why'd you risk everything to shoot that Harvester Robot?"

"Why, why it was the right thing to do."

"Bingo, Matt. Same reason. You get it?" Matt looked at Camila. Then reached over and grabbed her hand.

"Yeah. I get it now. Thanks."

At that moment, James came back to the group with a big bag of dog food, two dishes and with Flash carrying a dog toy. He plunked down in the vacant seat. Raven haired Eve, seeing another attractive young man, smoothed her waitress uniform dress down again and came walking up with her best come-hither look once again.

"Hi! Another menu? Water?" Eve asked as she looked into James' eyes.

"Is Flash here okay? I mean I can..."

"He's not going to pee on the floor, is he? Other than that, I don't think anybody is going to complain, with the outside world nuts and all."

"Good!" replied James. "I want some pancakes. How about you all?"

"Steak and eggs, please Eve," said Camila. "My treat by the way." She placed a wad of bills on the table. "Or do you need something else in payment?"

The older waitress was walking up with a coffee pot and heard the question.

"Got a spare gun? We'll take that over cash these days."

"That can be arranged, Miss..."

"Just call me Ruby. My man Joe is the cook. Steak and eggs all around, with some pancakes on the side. As I said, we have to get rid of some food before we lose power and it all goes bad." Ruby reached down and scratched Faith's ears. "Nice dog."

Ruby and Eve made sure the group's meal was just right. The four had forgotten how hungry they were until the food was set down. Then they inhaled it, with James sneaking snacks to Flash every chance he got. When the meal was over, Camila pushed herself back from the table.

"Best meal in…I can't remember when. I could get fat eating here."

"Do we stay here?" asked James.

"You can. With Eve there. She'll take care of you."

"Hey, Camila, don't give my brother away just yet!"

"What I'm trying to say is, with me, duty calls. If you three think you can make it here, in a small town, have at it. I don't think things will ever be the same again." The three young companions looked at each other.

James spoke up first. "I want to join up. Like Father. I want to… stop that Squids from killing any more of my Family. Like Father, Mother, Uncle Mark, and Sally," James told them.

Janice had started to protest but then fell silent. She

reached across the table and grasped her brother's hand. "It won't be easy, Brother. But if you want to, I'll support you." Janice looked at Matt.

"I'll fight also," Matt said. "I thought about joining up before all this... happened." Matt looked at Janice. She reached over and squeezed his hand.

"I'd wait for you, Matt. I'm not the military type, but I'll find something worthwhile to do."

Sergeant Camila Sanchez sat quietly, looked at these three young people, remembered back to when she ran off and joined up. But that was different. There were no space rocks, thinks falling from the sky to kill innocent people, creatures finding ways to hunt, kill and eat humans. Now, it was all so... personal. Especially after the Blackhawk shoot down and then Sally.

"Richards effing Raiders," Camila blurted out. "Damn, that fits now. What say we go looking for some sushi and calamari?" The four laughed until Flash began to bark and snarl at someone across the room.

"What is it, Flash?" James said as he held onto the new leash he had bought him. Camila looked up and froze. A being who fit the previous description of Mister Strange to a 'T' had just walked into the restaurant. Eyes a bit too far apart, odd shaped skull. He could pass as human if you didn't know any better. But Richards Raiders all knew better. And Flash had just confirmed it.

With Mr. Strange were three thugs. One had his face and body covered with prison tattoos, and his pants looked like prison issue. This man sneered at the group.

"Better curb your dog before someone does it for you." None of the four responded. Mr. Strange called out to Ruby with this odd Queens English accent.

"May we have some service, please?"

"Are you eyeing us, people?" One of the other slugs spat at them. "You dissin us?"

Camila broke their alleged trance with a loud voice. "Remember that movie with Denzel Washington? Book of Eli? The scene where he said things were so bad you could smell hijackers a mile away?" As she spoke, her hand slid under her fatigue blouse and slid the M-17 out. "Well, things are so bad now you can smell a Squid Lover a mile away."

Sergeant Sanchez had the pistol out and shot before she thought anyone else in the group would notice, But James had let go of Flashes leash and pulled his handgun out at the same time. Flash belied the non-aggressive nature of greyhounds by going straight for Mister Strange, who let out this odd keening scream as the K-9 latched onto his groin. The three thugs were down with bullet holes in their heads and other parts before anyone else realized what was happening. James was up and walking like an automaton towards Mr. Strange as the being tried to fight off Flash.

As Camila yelled "NO!" Janice caught up with James and grabbed him in a bear hug. He stopped advancing. Matt was then out front and yanked Flash off of the alien being. Mr. Strange tried to speak in English, but some other odd accented language kept interfering.

Camila moved up and had her pistol inches from the being's face.

"Gotcha, asswipe."

It took a few minutes for the group to explain what the hell had just happened in Ruby's Restaurant. A local aged constable showed up, took one look at what had happened, and let Sergeant Sanchez take charge. Matt fueled up the HUMVEE as Janice kept Mr. Strange covered after they had tied him up. Camila paid Ruby and Eve with three pistols taken off of the dead thugs/prison escapees, plus a wad of bills as a tip. James kept petting Flash and saying "Good dog, good dog," until Camila told him it was time to go, *now*. Raven-haired Eve gave her hero such a kiss that James would never forget it. Then they were out and drove away.

Mr. Strange kept trying to insist it was all a misunderstanding, that he just had some birth defects, that he would sue them for treating a disabled person this way, etcetera, etcetera. Flash kept trying to bite him in the cramped confines of the HUMVEE, so the ride for the being was not pleasurable. Ruby said she would keep trying to raise Malmstrom on the telephone, but it was not working, so it was up to the group to try and get him there in one piece. Matt drove as fast as he could *and* still keep the vehicle on the road. Eventually Mr. Strange stopped trying to convince them the errors of their ways and instead quietly sat as Flash glowered at him.

The group was about to cross the Dearborn River, some sixty miles from Malmstrom when they realized they may have a problem they had not foreseen. Janice had been periodically standing up through the HUMVEE roof hatch and using the binoculars to scan the area and look for aerial activity. They kept hoping that Ruby or someone would get through to Malmstrom and a Blackhawk or some another helicopter would meet them on the road. Instead, Janice called out "Houston, we have a problem."

"Janice, what's up?" Camila Asked.

"I think we have a Delta trying to line up on us—it's coming in at a very high altitude. I just got a flash of sunlight on metal."

"Someone said at McChord that the Deltas came in from a suborbital altitude. They have some kind of launching and landing platforms in low orbit."

"Well, now what?" Mister Strange picked that moment to start talking again. "If you let me go, you may live. If you do not, we will all die. My masters will kill me rather than have my kind captured."

"Yeah?" said Camila. "And what kind is your kind?"

"I am from an ancestor of yours. We are related. I was

created from pre-Homo sapiens genetic material. So, you will be killing a relative."

Camila laughed. "I guess you people haven't studied us enough. We had Royal Cousins declaring war on each other in World War One."

"Uh, people?" Janice said. "Decision time."

"Camila, there looks like an old abandoned homestead over there to our right, See it?" Matt asked.

"Yes, Matt. That looks like a barn. Try hiding in it," Camila responded.

Matt drove the HUMVEE across the fields and then through a set of broken down barn doors. He shut off the engine, and they all sat.

"Damn. This is not going to work," Camila said.

"Why not?" asked Janice.

"They tracked him here, they can track him in this barn."

"Well, Camila. What's the next idea?" Matt asked.

"Stinger," James said.

"Yes, James," Camila agreed. "That is an option. But we get only one shot."

"Or we get blown up in a barn for sure."

"Dammit, James. There are times I wish you were not so analytical."

Camila and Matt dug the Stinger Missile from the back of the HUMVEE. The Sergeant talked to her self as she remembered the loading and launch sequence.

"Damn, I fired one of these things two years ago. First I get shot down by one of these things, now I have to use one."

"Camila," Janice called out from the edge of the barn. "The Delta is descending."

Camila found a missing part of the wall in the back of the ramshackle barn. She stepped out and tried to detect the Delta with the Stinger Infra-Red Sight. As she did, she heard James behind her.

"This will be only a temporary solution."

"What?

"They will send a Falcon if the Delta is destroyed. We cannot defeat a Falcon."

Camila began to use curse words even she did not think she knew. "So we let him go," Camila said.

"Yes... and no."

The four low crawled from the barn. The group self-named as Richards Raiders had grabbed as many supplies, in including weapons as they could. Slowly the HUMVEE backed out from the barn thanks to a found brick wedged on the gas pedal. Tied and gagged in the back seat was a distraught Mister Strange who was missing a thumb and forefinger. Camila had taken them so the scientists and Intelligence people they finally contacted could figure out just what he was. The HUMVEE kept backing across the field as the Delta came screeching in on a gunnery run. The hypervelocity cannons spat, and the two shells tore through the side of the vehicle. Mr. Strange's body was eviscerated and immolated as two forty millimeter grenades rigged to the spare jerry can of fuel exploded. The burning HUMVEE also gave more of a fireworks display when two road flares spit out there contents. The Delta took one more low altitude pass to ensure the area around where the being had died was a mass of flames. Then it accelerated straight up and away.

"Sons of bitches are too smart," cursed Matt.

"They have had decades to plan, Matt. We have not," James stated.

"Well, we need a vehicle for my bum leg," said Camila. "Unless we want to spend the rest of this Invasion homesteading on an abandoned farm. Or is it a ranch?"

"I think the fireworks may attract someone, even if there are no current Missile Launch Control Facilities out in this area," stated James.

"Uh oh," said Janice. "Brushfire, and I think it will spread to that barn."

The four managed to make to the paved State Road 200. There they sat and planned. As much as they could, with no prospects of transportation. About an hour later, a single horse rider came across the fields and plains. It was a young girl, about twelve years old and she approached the group cautiously. Janice stood up and walked to meet her.

"Nice looking horse," Janice called out.

"Thanks," replied the young girl. "That your burnt car? "

"Yes. It was a HUMVEE. A Squid Delta got it."

"So those fast jets are some kind of flying saucers? Space aliens?"

"Yes. Have you gotten any emergency broadcasts out here?"

"No, Ma'am. Our satellite dish went out last week. Radio went out not long after that."

"Well, we have a sergeant over there with a hurt leg. We need to get her to Malmstrom Air Force Base. Can you help us? By the way, my name is Janice."

"I'm Emily. Please to meet you. I'll get the wagon."

The four survivors were in the back of a slow-moving wagon pulled by a tired horse. The four companions talked with Emily on the way to her small ranch house on the banks of the Dearborn River.

"Mom has been gone for a year. Dad went to Great Falls last week. The phones went out, I haven't heard from him since. I saw all these odd looking jets zipping around. Then the Flying Saucers showed up. I hid."

"Smart move, Emily," said Camila.

"Yeah. My Dad said not to trust strangers out here. We rarely see the Sheriff."

"Where's school?" James asked.

"I bounced around to the small schools around here until two years ago when Mom started homeschooling me. Then last year she died, Dad started trying to sell the place then. He went to town as he had an offer to buy. Those alien crafts came, and he never returned."

"You have food, water, heat?" Matt asked.

"Yes. Dad always kept lots of extra for when we have a bad winter and get snowed in, We have a small gas generator as well as some solar panels that charge some batteries we have."

"You don't get lonely out here?" Asked Janice.

"No. I have my 4-H friends. My church friends. I can ride a horse to the neighbors. I'll be 13 next year. If I'm back in school, I'll make new friends."

"What's your last name?" Asked Matt

"Anderson."

The ranch house and outbuildings of Emily's home were well built and taken in good repair. Camila limped in and sat on the living room sofa as Emily made everyone some hot tea.

"I like tea," Emily said. "Got that from my Mom."

"Mind if I look around?" Matt asked"

"Go ahead. If you could wipe my horse down, I'd appreciate it."

"Yeah, I'm used to that. My family also had some horses."

Emily soon served everyone tea and some cookies.

"I will make you some lunch if you want it."

"Later, honey," said Janice. "We had a large meal not too long ago."

"Okay." Emily walked back into the kitchen Matt walked into the house with a facial expression that said something was wrong."

"Ah, Camila. Can I get you to limp out here? There's something I think you need to see."

"Sure."

Five minutes later, Camila was standing with Matt in an outbuilding which was apparently a small blacksmiths shop. Emily's father was hanging from a noose thrown over a rafter.

"Think she knows?" Asked Matt.

"She saw it, then she didn't see it," replied Camila. "She's blocked it out." The Sergeant turned towards Matt. "We need to get her out of here. Her Father couldn't take all the loss. This could drive her over if she has to deal with it right now."

"Okay. I'll tell Janice and James."

Some snooping uncovered an older but serviceable SUV in a shed that served as a garage. There was also a horse trailer After a quick private conversation among the group members, Janice approached Emily.

"Hey, Emily. Your Dad left a spare vehicle out here. With a Horse Trailer. How's about we all take a trip to Great Falls and find your Dad? And then you could drop us off at the Air Force Base."

"Okay. I'll get some things."

The quickness in the response told Camila that Emily's young brain was trying to find a way out of an untenable situation. The fiction that Dad took a trip was a means for her to accept the horror of suicide.

People who commit suicide don't consider the effect it has on those who find them, thought Camila.

An hour later, thanks to Matt's skill with the horse and horse trailer, they were ready to go. Emily's Dad's body was wrapped in a tarp and concealed in the barn. The group did not have the time for burial, not to mention the effect that would have on Emily.

"We can come back?" Emily asked with childlike innocence from the backseat of the SUV.

"Of course we can," replied Matt. Emily smiled, then laid her head on Janice's shoulder and was out like a light.

"Her brain is trying to figure a way to deal with it all," whispered Camila. "Maybe a dream state will help."

"What about nightmares?" James asked.

"Wake her up if she starts crying or something like that. That should solve that problem."

The four figured they were about sixty miles from Great Falls and a few more to Malmstrom as it was on the east side of the city. Matt drove as usual, and they were soon making good time on State Rood 200. It was deserted until they hit Interstate 5 late that afternoon. Then signs of panic reappeared. Traffic was jammed on the way in and through Great Falls. Again, there was little sign of any type of law enforcement. Camila played with the Good Time Radio and finally found a working local AM station. The newscaster sounded as if he had been in the job for the last two days.

"Okay, people. Again. If you do not have to move, shelter in place. Great Falls is *not* a sanctuary. What little news we have from the federal government and what is left of any national media outlets is that the center of the United States is pretty damned safe. Can I say damn? Hell, no FCC. I can say the seven forbidden words. What's it going to do, eat me? The Tschaaa Aliens already have that down."

"Tschaaa. They have a name," James said.

"Sounds like their name also," added Camila. "Someone is talking with someone."

"Peace talks?" asked Janice.

"Why would some creature talk to their meal?" asked James.

As they slowly moved along, Camila noticed a cause for part of the traffic Jam. Some individuals could only be called a 'biker gang' were camped out on the interstate shaking down various vehicles. Camila and company saw them drag one driver out of his car, turn him upside down and shake the valuables out of his pockets.

"I thought Montanans usually pack heat," commented Camila.

"I guess some don't. Or there could be Canadians in the mix." Matt edged the SUV forward, trying to avoid the miscreants. Unfortunately, two of them walked towards the SUV.

"Guns," said Camila.

"Where ya going?" A scraggly bearded man shoved his face into the passenger side window. He quickly had an M-17 pistol screwed into his left nostril courtesy of a Staff Sergeant Sanchez.

"None of your business, Stinky." Three other pistols were soon pointed out the SUV various windows. A couple of more observant members of the biker group began to deploy what appeared to be formerly U.S. Military weapons, and Camila yelled out. "Keep that up, and you will be wearing a couple of your buddies brains as your new colors. After that, you will have extra ventilation holes in your respective bodies."

"We are your worse nightmare," James said in his best imitation Terminator voice.

The bikers glared at the group as their SUV passed, having decided discretion was the better part of valor in this case. Or that 'Richards Raiders' just were not worth it. Both Janice and Camila flashed them their best crap-eating grins. Emily slept the sleep of the exhausted innocent.

nce past the bikers, traffic speed pick up a bit.

"Look for signs to the base," said Camila.

"You have never been here?" asked James

"Hey, being in the United States Air Force does not mean you get a grand tour of all the air bases. Just look for a sign that says 'Malmstrom AFB This Way,' and it will be fine."

A few minutes later they were off on the State Highway 200 spur, and a sign stated Malmstrom was ahead.

"Okay. Hide your guns. Let me do the talking."

Malmstrom Air Force Base Maingate had been turned into an armored and sandbagged blockhouse. A heavy fifty caliber machine gun tracked the SUV as Matt drove ever so slowly forward. Two armed Security Force personnel approached them with M-4s at Low Ready. The female member called out something feet from the vehicle.

"ID and show me your hands please."

"Air Force Staff Sergeant Camila Sanchez, Pararescue,

McChord Air Force Base, Washington. These others are friends and family."

The Female Senior Airman walked up and spent a full minute examining Camila's ID and Restricted Area Badge. She handed the items back to Camila.

"Sorry, Sergeant, but we have found out you can't be none too careful." A hint of a smile formed on the woman's mouth. "You look like you've been through the wringer."

"You don't know the half of it. In fact, my friends and I have some information your Intelligence people will find interesting. We had some face-time close up and personal with some Squids and their minions."

The Senior Airman's eyes widened a bit. "You saw a Squid? Close up?"

"We killed a couple. And some robots." James said with a grin.

"You all have weapons?" the Security Policewoman asked.

"Yes. And I have government-issued weapons," replied Camila.

"Okay, Staff Sergeant. Follow the Sergeant over there. You check the personal weapons over at that large connex. You can carry issued small arms as we have already had problems with infiltrators."

"Thank you, Senior Airman... Tibbs. Hope to see you again."

"Likewise," she replied to Camila with a grin. Tibbs stepped back and saluted the SUV as Matt drove it past.

"I thought you saluted Officers," said James.

"I guess she saw that we are Richards Raiders," Camila said with a grin.

Tibbs or someone must have made some telephone calls as soon a harried-looking young Captain showed up at the connex as the group checked their weapons in. The Stinger Missile raised eyebrows. Standing a bit behind the Captain was a tall and wiry dark-haired man in urban camos and sunglasses. With her Fritz helmet back on and her Uniform as squared away as possible after living in it for a week, Camila saluted the Captain.

"Sir, Staff Sergeant Camila Sanchez…"

"Sergeant, belay that. I should salute you. Instead, I'd like to shake your hand."

"Sir?"

"I understand you and your friends had some up close and personal time with the Tschaaa as we now know them and their minions. Oh, I'm Captain Dreger, Intelligence Unit here. This is Special Agent John Leer, from Washington D.C."

"What's left of it, Sergeant," interjected the Agent.

"Yes. And the Agent and I need to debrief you all. First, I have arranged some temporary quarters for you all in Base Housing. We are putting you all in a vacant house there so you will be left alone. All the barracks and temporary quarters are jammed up anyways. So, we'll escort you all to the quarters first, let you clean up, get some chow. Then, we need to talk to you… all."

"Can I stay with them?' An awake Emily asked. "I lost my Dad."

Captain Dreger gave Camila a quizzical look.

"She helped us get here, Captain. We kind of… adopted her into our tribe."

"That has been happening a lot lately," commented Agent Leer.

"Of course. Your dog also. We'll sort out the details later." The Captain motioned to a pair of Senior Airman. "They'll get you to your temporary quarters. We'll try to rustle up some clothes also. Again, let me shake your hands. All of you. Heroes like you will help save us."

"Captain, here." Camila handed a plastic baggy with a thumb and forefinger in it.

"Piece of some being the Squids brought along who

looks a bit like us. They stopped us from bringing the whole body."

The Captain stood and stared.

As Matt drove the SUV and followed the Security Police Vehicle after dropping off Emily's horse at some stables, he commented, "That Captain seemed more like a customer service representative than an Intelligence Officer."

"Well, Matt, things are screwed up. And he may be schmoozing us so we will be more pliable," replied Camila.

James spoke up. "Who cares? We tell them what we know, what happened."

Camila turned and looked at James. "Tell him, James, that you had to shoot some people. Do not go into a lot of details. Tell them it happened fast and was all blurry. I don't think you and Janice want your brains picked apart."

"Okay. My wire is not loose right now," James replied.

"Good. Let's keep it that way."

The house in the Base Housing Area had been a Senior Non Commisioned Officers Family Quarters. Someone had fitted it out with clean bedding, towels, and washcloths. Emily sacked out again as the others quickly took showers with heavenly hot water.

Before that, Camila had slipped Matt a sidearm. *"Spare military issue. Keep it hidden, though."*

"You don't trust somebody?"

"Other than you three and Emily, I don't trust anyone right now."

There was a small awkward moment when Matt caught Janice in nothing but a towel. He blushed and started to turn away.

"Matt," said Janice.

"Ah, yeah?"

"If I were older than sixteen I'd suggest we shower

together. But I think, right now…"

"It would cause problems. I know. We'll… talk later."

"I'd like that," Janice said with a grin.

Some civilians, maybe military dependents being put to work, brought over a bunch of hot chow hall food as well as a menagerie of clothes. Someone guessed at Camila's size and brought her a new set of BDUs, with E-6 Tech Sergeant Stripes sewed on.

"Some computer records are working," Camila mused. It made her feel good.

As soon as everyone was showered and dressed in clean clothes, they all sat down to eat. The Sun was setting as Emily asked to say, Grace. "Thank you. God, for getting us here. Thank you for my new family. Thank you for this food. In Jesus Name, Amen."

The group did not talk much as they stuffed their faces with the lovely, hot food. Matt did comment on how he thought military chow was supposed to be awful, but this wasn't. That sparked a bit of laughter and smiles. The group kept eating until everyone was sufficiently satiated. They all helped clean the dishware up, and next went to sit in the living room. Someone had thrown a few books and magazines around the house, but that was it. There was no TV or radio.

"Sequestered," Camila said. "I think they sequestered us."

"That is because they need to make sure we are who we say we are," said James.

"I think you hit that on the head, James," commented Matt.

"Are things that screwed up?" asked Janice.

"I think so," Matt said. "Look at the guy who tried to take our HUMVEE. Or that 'fake' human we tried to bring here. It is going to take a long time to sort all of this mess out."

There was a knock on the front door. Camila rose and answered it. Standing on the porch in the waning light was Captain Dreger.

"Sergeant, I hope you have all had a shower and some good food."

"Yes, Sir. Thank you. And I bet now is the time we get talked to."

"All but the young girl called Emily. I have a young female Airman to stay with her. The rest, I have a large SUV to drive you to the Intelligence Office."

"Okay, Captain. One minute please." Camila went to the living room, whispered a few last minute instructions and collected the group.

"Okay, Captain. Lay on McDuff."

They kept the four survivors separated as they were being interviewed. For some reason, Camila was called in last. At least she assumed all the others were finished with their interviews as she saw them being led one by one to a small holding area with refreshments. Then the Senior Airman came for her. She walked into the small office and saw Agent Leer sitting behind the desk.

"Sir, Technical Sergeant...

"You can belay that, Sergeant, I am not Military. Please have a seat." Leer smiled as Camila sat down. "You know, I recently interviewed this Marine Corps Gunnery Sergeant. Tough as nails he was. I had almost to order him to sit down." The Agent frowned. "Then halfway through I had to tell him his younger brother had just been killed. Died a hero, one of the first and many. But I still had to tell him he lost family."

He fixed Camila with a stare. "So how many have you lost?"

Sergeant Camila Sanchez took a deep breath, then let it out. "I haven't been close to my blood family for some time, so I don't know how many have been killed this past week," Camila said. "But I lost my PJ Family when the Blackhawk was shot down by a bunch renegades, effing traitors."

"Yes," said Leer. "The others had some interesting details to pass on." Leer shuffled some papers, looked at one page in particular.

"The so-called leader talked like he had a special relationship with this Mr. Strange character and through him, with the Aliens, we now know call themselves the Tschaaa."

"Yes, Sir. He talked about being paid in money and sexual favors."

"Yes, Sergeant, quite a despicable character." Agent Leer shuffled some more papers around. "Then your friends started killing them."

Camila began to wonder just what this Agent really wanted. What did he expect, given the circumstances? "Sir, I was bleeding like a stuck pig, and being taken to be porked by two smelly a-holes. So the fact they killed a bunch, so what? They were going to shoot James for talking back." Camila tried to control her temper, as she knew the Agent was just trying to push her buttons to get a reaction. But she was still human. "I tried to kill two of them myself."

"And according to the others, James helped finish them off, execution style," said Leer. "Yet, supposedly, all three of these civilians were just average teenagers, playing in the woods when the Tschaaa show up."

The Agent pulled another page out from his files.

"Then you all had another series of adventures, to include losing a member of the group to a couple of Squids which popped out of the Spokane River. Next, a shootout at a small restaurant in Montana where you kill three more people and grab this, what we now call Front Men for the Aliens, as a prisoner. However, you lose him…"

"Those are his digits I gave you," interrupted Camila. Leer pulled another paper out and continued talking.

"I will have to admit that is rather interesting. You know what the preliminary DNA exam reveals on him?"

"I have not a clue," Camila responded.

"He is not Homo sapiens, that is for sure. Some anthropologist suggested a direct link to Homo erectus. You know what that suggests?"

"Again, Sir, not a clue."

"Someone from out there visited us way before Roswell, New Mexico." Agent Leer leaned back in his chair and steepled his fingers. He kept looking at Camila. He then finally spoke. "You friend James has quite an analytical mind on him, you know that?"

"Yes, Sir. He can definitely figure things out."

The Agent took a cell phone from his pocket, and began to scroll through the photos in the memory. "Now convince me how these photos on his phone are not fake."

Camila exploded. She stood up, started to advance on the Agent but stopped herself. Through clenched teeth, she hissed. "In those photos are Sally Card. U.S. Forest Service Employee, her severed head and body. You think we faked those, buddy?"

Agent Leer sat in his chair, seemingly ignoring Camila as he kept looking through the photos in James' cell phone. "Lucky we got these when we did, Sergeant." He finally said. " The battery was about dead. We might have lost some of the data." He looked up at Camila. "So, are you going to waste time kicking my ass, or do you want to kick some Squid Ass?"

Camila had no idea how to answer, She just sat back down, silent. Agent Leer leaned forward across the desk to speak. "You know, that Marine almost kicked my ass, too. You know I get paid to try and get people to kick my ass? You know a couple of times I really got smacked?" Leer laughed. "Yes, you know that I push buttons. I push people's buttons. You know why?"

"Haven't a clue," Camila answered.

"To see if I am being fed bullshit, Sergeant. Peacetime, I have more time to figure things out. Then the bullshit might not hurt someone. Today, right this second, bullshit is killing people." Leer leaned back in his chair again. "We have these Front Men and Quislings, traitors and renegades, spreading all types of misinformation as well as committing sabotage and assassination. Why a human being would side with an alien species, I have no idea. But they are. So I have to make sure every person who comes in here with a story that seems too good to be true is vetted. Not just vetted but gone through with a fine tooth comb. Or sliced up with a scalpel."

The two humans sat quietly for a moment, looking at each other. Finally, Camila spoke.

"Am I free to go, Sir?"

"From this interview, yes," replied Leer. "From this invasion, this war, no. You and your friends will be called on to do more in the coming years. I say years because all the info we have are that the Squids may be here to stay." Agent Leer began stuffing papers back into a file folder. "So, go back to the house they put you up in. The Powers That Be will be deciding how to use you, just as they use me, Sergeant. We are cogs in a big machine, But we are necessary if humankind is to remain on this planet we call Mother Earth."

Camila stood up, said "Have a nice night," turned and left. She did not look back. The Sergeant limped and went to find her New Family. She wanted to spend one decent night with them before reality came crashing in again; the real, real world of dead friends, comrades, and decapitated heads.

She found Matt, James, and Janice in this spare room with refreshments. She noticed there was alcohol there, poured herself a still bourbon and drank it. She then turned to her Family.

"What say we go home and have a good sleep?" Camila asked them.

"Sounds good to me," Matt responded.

"How'd it go?" asked Janice.

Camila shrugged. "I guess he is doing a job no one really

likes. I guess because everything is going to hell in a handbasket, it has to be done."

"I had a fascinating conversation with Agent Leer," James interjected.

"You did?" Matt asked

"Why yes," replied James. "He tried to give me a form of Third Degree. You know, like the old movies. All rough and tough. Acted as if I was a liar, or crazy."

"Did he talk about your cell phone photos?" asked Camila.

"Of course. Agent Leer tried to yell at me, tell me the photos were fake. That we made all these stories up to be special."

"So, what did you do?" Asked Janice.

"I laughed at him." The three companions stared at him.

"You laughed at him?" Asked Camila.

"Why, yes," said James. "He has no real power over me. What can he do? Kill me and eat me? We have already been faced by that. The Tschaaa will do that if we are not careful. But if they did, it would be quick. They are predators, not torturers."

"And you know that how?" asked Janice.

"Just analyze their actions. If they were torturers, why would they care about dead bodies? They would spend more time trying to catch us alive if they received pleasure from torturing. Instead, that use methods that usually kill. Like with the harpoons, the Deltas. And of course, the rock strikes. If they were into torture, they would be like those alien abduction stories. With the anal probes and such. They grab us, alive or dead, it does not matter. They may slaughter us like a side of beef, but it is all about them eating us, not watching us suffer."

"How about the people they hire? Those renegades?" asked Camila

James paused in thought for a while, a frown on his face. "I think they believe they understand us better than they really do. The Squids, the Tschaaa believe they can control some of us and use them against other humans. However, I have this impression their culture is different than most of ours. They are straight predators. Those two Squids who killed Sally. They were trying to prove something by hunting with weapons from their past. They killed her quick. They had no capture implements like nets. They were out for meat."

The three survivors looked at James as all he said sank in. Matt whistled. "You definitely have an analytical mind, James," stated Matt. "Did you express some of these thoughts to Leer?"

"Oh yes," answered James. "He stopped trying to browbeat me and began to listen. I think he realizes that our actual experiences can help the government fight the Tschaaa. Maybe to find a way to communicate with them. If we talk to them, maybe we can reason with them."

Camila laughed. "And why would they want to talk to a side of beef? We are for eating, not for dinner conversation. Can you imagine talking 'turkey' at Thanksgiving as you get ready to carve the bird up?"

"That is a valid point, Camila. But we used to eat dogs in the U.S. Now we talk and communicate with them all the time. We use them as service animals, but we still love them. And they love us. Like Flash."

"So we could be 'service animals' to them. At least some of us," Camila said. She snorted. "I cannot see myself as the Squid's best friend."

The next couple of days the group including Emily were allowed to kick back and relax at their assigned house. They offloaded all their supplies still in the SUV and rearranged those items plus all the items given to them by the Base. Just having the same bed to sleep in every night was a luxury, not to mention hot water. Camilla received a call from the local Pay and Finance Office and was told she would be receiving pay and benefits of an E-6 Technical Sergeant. The payment included Combat Pay as every place on Earth was now a Combat Zone thanks to an Alien Invasion. She signed up James, Emily, and Janice as dependents since they were under eighteen years of age. Camila decided it would be pushing the envelope to sign up Matt as an eighteen-year-old as a dependent. He understood and went out looking for a job. Which there were many involving physical labor due to all the damage in and around the Base thanks to rock and aerial attacks by Deltas. A little bit of snooping and Camila soon found out that a couple of good-sized rocks had smashed into Malmstrom Air

Force Base proper. The airfield had been reduced in size over the years and had been used primarily for rotary aircraft in support of the Intercontinental Ballistic Missile Field. Deltas and Falcons had only attacked a couple of the Launch Control Facilities, so it was assumed all the missiles were capable of retaliatory launch. But against who?

It was the morning of the third day on Base and there was knock on the front door. Camila answered it, limping with her pistol hidden behind her right thigh. Agent Leer had said figuring out who to trust was a problem. Upon opening it, there was the young Senior Airman Tibbs who had checked her in the Main Gate.

"Excuse me, Sergeant, but there is a meeting at the Wing Headquarters Building at 1300 hours. They would like you and any members of your group available to attend. In this large envelope are I.D. passes for y our party."

"Do you know what it's about, Airman Tibbs?"

"First Name is Lisa, Sergeant," Tibbs said with a smile. "The rumor mill is that you are one of the few with extensive contact with the enemy forces on a face-to-face basis. But please don't say I told you. I think its supposed to be a surprise."

"My lips are sealed, Lisa. And I'm Camila. Us NCOs need to stick together. Thank you. See you soon, I hope."

"Likewise, Lisa." There was that beautiful smile from a good looking blonde woman again. Camila realized she may have to decide how 'confused' she really was. Well, time to contact the others.

Matt was working so Camila had to drive over and find him. She explained to the work party supervisor she needed to borrow him and the Sup readily agreed.

"You killed some Squids close up," the beefy man stated.

"Yes, we did. And some of their renegade helpers."

"Putter there, Sarge," the man said as he shook her

hand. "You'll never have to pay for beer when I'm around."

That was the reaction all of the group was beginning to receive. The word about the adventures was spreading like wildfire. So much for Communications Security.

One o'clock. Camila, Matt, James, and Janice were at the Wing Headquarters Building. Emily was with a tutor/counselor who was dealing with the whole "Dad's missing" subject. The Sergeant had convinced the three 'youngsters' to dress in the best clothes they had, which was pretty good thanks to the largess of strangers when they had first arrived on Malmstrom. They were escorted into the Wing Briefing Room as if they were dignitaries. When she saw Agent Leer siting with the ranking Commanders, she knew why. This could be a good thing or a bad thing, she thought. Camila whispered to James as they were led to their seats.

"Answer just what they ask, simply. No pontifications." James nodded 'yes.'

A General Samuel Smith was the senior officer, To his right was a General Reed who looked like he had a brand new set of stars on his shoulders. Battlefield promotion? Could be with so many of the military killed in the first few days.

My God, Camila thought. *Just over a week and it seems like forever.*

Sitting in the same area as Camila and the others was a man with Hollywood good looks and a Marine Corps Uniform with Gunny Stripes and fruit salad that went all the way up his chest.

Damn, she thought, *he's been around for being so young looking.*

After all the required introductions, pomp and circumstance, they got down to the nitty-gritty. General Smith laid the groundwork. "We asked you to come here, especially you civilians, as you are some of the first survivors to have personal contact with our enemy. Or should I say, enemies? We have Marine Corps Gunnery Sergeant Torbin Bender, USAF Technical Sergeant Camila Sanchez and her three companions, Matthew Bearclaw, James Richards, and Janice Richards. Please allow me to express my condolences as I know all of you have lost family members these first few days. Based on the limited information we have so far, millions more will be lost, primarily in the coastal areas."

The General continued.

"Because of the high casualty rate, we are working against a time clock never faced before in the history of the world. For we could easily reach the point where major governments break down all at once, and civilization as we know it grinds to a halt."

"General John Reed, you just barely made it out of Washington D.C. Can you tell us what was happening worldwide?"

The former USAF pilot sat for a moment before speaking.

"D.C. is gone; there is a Harvester Ark on the White House lawn. Those wheeled robots are grabbing and butchering people by the thousands."

There was murmuring among the people seated around the significant participants. Noticing this, General Reed motioned to the Marine Gunnery Sergeant.

"Gunnery Sergeant Bender. You survived the counter-attack on the Yuma Overpass and the destruction of a Harvester Arc. Can you explain what you saw before you blew the craft up?"

"General, it was a huge mobile slaughterhouse. Human slabs of meat hung everywhere."

Somebody, probably a local official, cried out. "This can't be happening."

"It is. And to children," replied Gunny Bender. Somebody left the meeting in a hurry. The thought of kids being eaten by outer space creatures did not sit well with lunch.

"Technical Sergeant Sanchez."

"Yes, General Smith." Camila stood up as she spoke, trying to calm the butterflies in her stomach. Public speaking was not her foray.

"You and your compatriots killed a couple of these Squids close up. What say you about the enemy?"

"Sir, they are intelligent and dangerous predators who look on us as prey. But pump enough bullets into them, and they bleed and die like everything else. Bluish blood, but blood nevertheless."

There were some subdued positive comments, the word 'payback' was heard.

"Sir, may I speak?" It was James. Camila thought, *Oh great*, and tried to stare him down but he ignored her.

"You are James Richards, are you not?" General Smith said.

"Yes, sir."

"So you were with Sergeant Sanchez."

"Yes, Sir. Richards Raiders." James comment led to some light laughter. *But that was probably a good thing though*, Camila thought as she sat down. At least she hoped.

"Well, Son, what would you like to add?"

James took a deep breath, then let it out. He scanned the room with eyes that seemed to see everything. Then he began to speak

"General, my Father and Mother died for my sister Janice and I. They died fighting alien robots like out of some science fiction movie, but it was no movie. Then Matthew Bearclaw," he said, motioning to Matt, "he came along and saved us also. The three of us fled Darrington, Washington. We made our way away from a vast Harvester Ark that had landed and took our parents. Then we met the late Forest Service Employee Sally Card, she helped us get away form Deltas and Falcons, alien craft thing in their capabilities. But we made it, dodged the Squids." James paused, swallowed, and began again. "Then, when we thought we were being saved, when Sergeant Sanchez came along in a Blackhawk with a bunch of other PJs. Then the unthinkable happened." James scanned the room again.

"Other humans shot down the Blackhawk. Humans who were helping the Tschaaa harvest and butchered us. The leader said they did it for sex, money, and power. Humans. Helping aliens eat us. What can be more sick and evil than that? The Tschaaa see us as cattle, meat. As we look at the animal, we eat. We are not evil because we eat flesh. It is part of our evolution. But what is evil is a human helping another creature eat one of their own, forcing people like me to kill those humans to survive." James paused as if in thought, then continued.

"We need to fight the Tschaaa, to convince them it is not worth it to try and eat us. But to me as important, is to eradicate the renegade humans who help the Squids to harvest us. To me, that is an even greater evil." James sat down. There were a few claps, more murmurs.

"The young man makes a very valid point. For we have had acts of sabotage on this Base. Humans begin to distrust each other even more than they have in the past. Thus, we have another front to deal with."

Camila wished James had not spoken when he did. It removed the emphasis on who started all the problems in the first place. If not for the Squids, there would be no renegade humans. Take the Tschaaa out, the renegades lose their power.

The meeting went on for another hour. Camila had thought something more substantial would come out, but it was the same message. Fight, but with conflicting ideas as to how. Camila knew enough that unless a real leader emerged, people would stumble around until a Tschaaa wound up on their doorstep. Then many would panic, run screaming. Suddenly, gloom descended over her, and she wondered if maybe they could have made life on Emily's Ranch after they got rid of her Dad's body. The memory of his hanging body made her think of Sally Card, then of her dead PJs, then... Her mode began to spiral down into depression.

"Hey, Sergeant. You have a dark cloud forming." Camila jerked back to the here and now. It was Gunny Bender. He had a smile on his face, but his blue eyes were intense, almost piercing.

"Oh. Sorry, Gunny. Woolgathering."

"Woolgathering? Well, unless you plan on knitting a sweater, I can tell you from years of experience, it does you no good. For I am a wool gatherer par excellence. Just ask my former commanders and girlfriends." His tenor and way of speaking made Camila laugh in spite of her self. Part of the laughter was picturing Bender knitting a sweater in Marine dress blues. "You are picturing me knitting a sweater now, aren't you?"

Camila laughed some more at being caught picturing that absurdity. She stuck her hand out as still smiled. "We have not been formally introduced. Camila."

"Torbin," the Marine said as he gave her a firm handshake. "Now that we have been introduced, I invite you to the NCO club for some libations."

"Ah, I have to get home with my family…"

"I'll drive them home," interrupted Matt. "I got them here."

"You must be Matt Bearclaw," said Torbin.

"You know that because the General introduced me," responded Matt. The two men shook hands.

"I thought about joining the Marines," said Matt.

"That might be kind of hard right now. Lejeune's and Paris Island are full of Squids. Not tasty calamari, but bear sized Squids. But why am I telling you that? You people have shot them."

"So, Camila," Matt continued, "I have Janice and James. You go visit with the Gunny and swap notes."

Camila looked at Matt and Janice and thought about them swapping something more than notes and almost refused.

She caught herself. They had all just faced death, and she was worried about some virginal sensibilities? What used to be considered underage sex now seemed the worse of their worries.

"Okay. Matt, you talked me into it. You have transport, Gunny?"

"If not, I can steal some."

"Then us having a drink together may be kind of hard if we are locked up in the stockade."

"Did I tell you I am a commensurate jailbreak artist also?"

It was nice to feel the camaraderie of some fellow military types over a beer. Camila had felt like that idea was from a time ages ago, not just a week or two. She laid some cash on the bar and signaled the bartender for another beer when Torbin pushed the money back at her.

"I asked you here, I pay."

"Are you saying this is a date, Gunny?"

For once, Torbin seemed caught off guard. Then he laughed. "You want it to be? I hadn't thought of it that way, but…"

Camila knew she was getting a little bit tipsy in the old vernacular, on the way to drunk, then to sloppy sweaty sex smashed. She laughed at her own thought, reached over and grabbed the Marines belt buckle and pulled him to her.

"How about if I ask *you* out?"

"Out where?" Torbin asked back.

"Anywhere you want to go, Marine. You're fun. I need fun right now. I think you need some fun also."

"Young lady, you don't know the half of it."

"I'm not a lady. I am a PJ. We rescue people, sometimes from their virginity."

"Do I look like a virgin?" asked Torbin.

"No. But I almost did not come with you because I was worried about another person's virginity."

"Your young ward Janice, with Matt."

"Yes, but they almost died a couple of days ago. And have the start of something nice going. So why interfere?" She noticed those blue eyes were looking into her again. "You see something nice inside of me, Marine?"

"Yes. You are a good soul, Camila Sanchez. You care about others. Now, let's blow this place."

James and Emily were asleep when Janice snuck into Matt's bedroom. She shed the thin robe she had found and slid into bed with him. She kissed him and pushed up hard against his chest.

"You sure you want this?" asked Matt. "You're only sixteen."

"Almost seventeen. And my mother never knew this, but I was not a virgin. I had a one afternoon stand at a friend's house. With her brother."

"Why?"

"To feel something good."

"Did you... feel good?"

"Yes."

She kissed him, and everything else faded away.

Camila woke up at o'dark-thirty in the morning. She was pressed up against Torbin Benders broad back. She took in his definite man scent and enjoyed it. She had discovered years ago in the military that people under the type of stress they experienced often used sex as a significant emotional release. Not to mention that many people in their career field became just plain horny. Well, she thought to herself, I'm not confused about what I like this morning. She stealthily slid out of bed and padded to the bathroom. Torbin had Senior NCO Bachelors Quarters, so he had a nice private toilet and shower. She relieved herself, then jumped into the shower. No sooner was she under the hot water than another body slid in.

"Save water, shower with a friend," said Torbin

"You know how old that expression is?" Camila asked.

"Older than I am. So I guess it makes it older than you. Or are you an old lady in disguise?"

She goosed him in a very sensitive part of his anatomy, and they laughed, then kissed. They broke the embrace when they realized one thing would lead to another, and they would never get out of the shower.

A quarter hour later, Camila and Torbin both had their uniforms on and ready to head out the door. She still had no official assignment. Camila thought that the powers that be were giving her a break until the figured out the four civilians who had attached themselves to her. The Sergeant would go back to her quarters and wait. The other limitation was her leg was still healing from the gunshot wound. The jacketed bullet had gone straight through, causing more bleeding than actual damage. However, even with a limp, she could still perform specific duties.

"Give me a ride?" Camila asked.

"Isn't that what we did last night?"

"Torbin Bender, you are such a smartass."

"Yep, and yep. Let's go."

Camila opened the front door of her on-base house and walked in. She smelled bacon cooking and went to the kitchen, James was making breakfast and had already scrambled some eggs.

"Eggs, Sergeant? My mother always fed them to us scrambled. They were easier to make. She had a career also as my father had."

Camila put some bread in the toaster and waited for the slices to pop up.

Janice walked into the kitchen drying her hair with a towel. "Good Morning. Sleep well, Sergeant?"

Camila couldn't help but laugh. "Hey, got something

private for you. Can you come to my room?"

"Okay, Camila."

In her room, Camila handed Janice a package of lubricated condoms. Janice blushed and began to stutter, which made Camila laugh.

"Look here, Janice. I may be a hardass at times when it comes to life and death things, but I am not your mother. And I was a wild child at your age. So birth control pills will soon disappear with many other pharmaceuticals as we fight this world war. Thus, be careful. Remember sex can be with or without love. Don't confuse the two." Janice looked at Camila, looked at the condoms, then hugged the older woman.

"Sorry, I'm so bitchy at times, especially when it comes to James."

"There is nothing wrong with protecting your brother. Now let's go eat. I'm starving."

The Base phone system was up and running so Camila made a few phone calls. She soon found out that the local authorities and Malmstrom Air Force Base were still trying to figure out what education would be like during the time of internal war. Emily was seeing a combination counselor and tutor due to her father's suicide, so she was taken care of for the time being. Matt had a job for at least some months. That left Janice and James. Having them sit around and dwell on things like the fact their parents were dead was not a good idea. Since Camila had some spare time, she would spend it setting them up for some type of education.

Someone knocked on the front door. Camila limped to it with her M-17 pistol ready. She opened it and saw Agent Leer standing there, dark sunglasses and all. He pointed to the gun.

"Going hunting?"

"Should I?" Camila answered. "What can I do for you, Agent Leer."

"I'd like to borrow James. Maybe permanently." The Sergeants mouth dropped open a bit. Then she spoke.

"Can you please take off the glasses? I need to see if your eyes are dilated due to drugs or psychosis."

Leer removed his glasses. "See. Normal. And I'm serious."

"Two questions," said Camila. "Why, and what's the catch. Or what's the catch and why. You pick."

"Your ward there has a very unique way of seeing things. He also analyzes the crap out of stuff we may deem unimportant. I need that right now."

"Why?" Camila asked again.

"In case you haven't noticed," Leer said sarcastically, "these things we call Squids—with a language, culture, and intelligence we do not understand—have invaded and are eating us. Plus, they are taking over the coastlines as well as bodies of water like the Great Lakes."

"And James can help figure that all out," said Camila.

"Why, yes. Because he thinks differently, James may help us figure out how these Aliens think. By the way. There are Lizards and Grey aliens we know next to nothing about. We need all the analytical help we can get."

Camila stood and thought for a moment. Then she replied. "I have some conditions."

"I expect you do. Just remember the military draft will be back. Soon."

"Okay. Leer. He gets paid a decent wage, and you treat him right. Anybody abuse him, I'll sick Matt Bearclaw on them. Oh, and he has to further his education."

"Want me to find him a wife also? "

"Hell, Agent Leer, can you?"

"Shake." The Agent put his hand out. Camila called for James.

"Yes, Sergeant?" said, James, as he walked up.

"Shake Agent Leer's hand if you want to be an Analyst

with him."

James paused for a moment, then shook hands. "Okay, Agent Leer. When do I start?"

"Tomorrow."

"Oh. One other thing," added Camila.

"Don't push a good thing, Sergeant," warned Leer.

"Janice needs a job, or training, or both. School may disappear as we know it."

Agent Leer sighed. "Yes. I think I can do that. But can I get something, Sergeant?"

"What's that?" Camila asked.

"If you are going to bend me over and pork me, can I at least have a kiss?"

16

amila used the lightweights as she strengthened her recovering injured leg. It felt to her that over the last two weeks, she had her leg back to the strength it was before she was shot. However, her physical therapist Jennifer Hutchins still pushed her.

"You were shot, Sergeant Sanchez. You may be a tough *chica* from El Paso, but you are not Super Woman."

"Yeah, yeah, yeah," Camila would respond back. Then her work out buddy, Janice, would get into it.

"If you think we're going to let you limp around the house and complain, you have another think coming." Things between her and Janice were going well after the little conversation with the condoms. Camila may feel like the Old Woman sometimes but at age 25, just some nine years older than her 'Ward' Janice, she really wasn't that much different. And like Camila had done, circumstances had forced Janice to 'grow up' quick. The fact that Agent Leer had found Janice a training program within the remains of whatever governmental

'Spook' agency he had come from had also helped. Janice and Matt were a couple. No one seemed to care about Janice's young age. Things like how old you are seem to matter less when someone is trying to eat you.

James was doing great. A couple of days after the 'handshake' with Agent Leer, James had pigeonholed Janice at the house.

"You were right, Sergeant Sanchez. I needed to be focused, to stay focused. This job makes me focus. There is no time for loose wires flopping around, no time to allow my personal problems to interfere. There are just time and the need to deal with the Tschaaa if we are to survive."

The meeting with Agent Leer had also led to Camila being ordered to physical therapy and then assigned to a reconstituted ParaRescue Unit on Malmstrom Air Force Base. Funny thing how she was one of the Senior NCOs as an E-6 and expected to help some of the newbies and get the Unit up and running.

It even allowed her some face-time, among other activities, with Master Gunnery Sergeant Torbin Bender. They were talking about officers rank for him due to the now famous Battle of the Yuma Overpass. He kept fighting the idea.

Camila and Torbin supplied a 'something' for each other, but there was not the feel of a permanent relationship. They would remain, friends, no matter where the relationship took them.

It would have been nice if the rest of the world was not going to hell in a handbasket. Just thirty days after the first rock hit the U.S., an Emergency Broadcast System Alert actually made it to all four corners of the United States. However, it said that there was no United States anymore. Ninety percent of the senior leadership was dead or in hiding. Everyone was on their own. Thus the former Strategic Missile Bases and other military installation in what was fly over country were trying to create some form of order.

That had happened just two days ago.

"That's it, Sergeant," Jennifer said. "That's enough workout for you today, good job."

"Thanks, Jennifer. Time to spend more time at work."

"Here are your next two appointments."

Camila walked away grumbling.

As she changed back into her uniform, Camila looked up and saw a gorgeous female body walking from the showers. She did a double take when she realized it was Senior Airman Lisa Tibbs who had first met the group at the Main Gate. Lisa saw Camila looking at her, threw her towel over the shoulder, so it covered just one beautiful boob and walked over.

"Hello, Sergeant Sanchez. You're looking a lot better this day."

Camila was lacing up her combat boots, so her face was about level with a specific blonde hair covered mound that denoted the female gender.

Camila started to stand up, and Lisa lightly put her hand on Camila's shoulder. She bent over a bit and said in a low voice, "If you like what you see, let's cut to the chase. I made Staff Sergeant. Come to help me celebrate. I'm in the telephone book." Lisa smiled, turned and walked away, her beautiful behind swaying just right.

"Oh, Lordy. I think I'm confused again," Camila whispered to herself.

Camila was at one of the rebuilt hangers looking over a newly recovered Blackhawk Helicopter when Torbin Bender walked up.

"Don't see many of these in one piece anymore," he said.

"No, Master Gunny, you don't. The Squids loved to blow up on air assets on the ground."

"My brother William got it in the air. But at least he took some of the enemies with him," Torbin stated.

"You were the Gunny Agent Leer told me about, weren't you? The one who almost kicked his ass, then he had to tell him his brother was lost."

"That be me, Sergeant."

"Well, Torbin," said Camila, "you did not come here for a trip down memory lane. What's up?"

" A mission. Agent Leers idea. And the Brass bought it."

"Which is, my friend?" asked Camila.

"We get to try and kidnap an alien," answered Torbin.

That night at home, Camila told the others—including Emily—that she would be away for a while. Hopefully, the time would be measured in days, but she could not be more specific for security reasons.

"Is it dangerous?" asked Emily.

"Of course it is," said James. "That's her job. Danger." Camila glared at James for once again being too damn blunt and then motioned to Emily.

"Come here and sit on your aunt's lap," requested Camila. Emily went over and sat on her lap.

"You're not really my Aunt, Camila. You know that. If my Dad were still alive, he'd tell you who my aunts are." What had happened to her father had finally been worked out with Emily. She now remembered he had killed himself, which still made her angry. But she would always love who he was before that.

"I know I'm not. But it is how our culture works out these things... nevermind. That is not the subject here. The subject is that I need to go away because of my Job. While I'm gone, Matt being the oldest will be in charge. But I'll have some other people check in. Here." She handed a large manila envelope to Matt.

"What's this?" Matt asked.

"Stuff you'll need if I... don't come back."

Janice began to blink back tears. "Oh come on, people.

We killed people together. You should be able to—"

"And we lost Sally," said James. "That hurt us all."

Camila had hoped she should get through this quick. However, no such luck.

"Who's going with you?" Janice finally said.

"Torbin Bender for one. Plus some other surviving PJs. We have scrounged up a Blackhawk helicopter for our ride."

"Torbin will get her back," James said. "I read his file."

"Did you read mine?" asked Camila.

"No. There is no reason to read yours. You've told us all about your life."

Camila sighed. James could be such a pain in the ass at times. "Okay. To cut this short, Matt's in charge. You, people, get to stay in this house for the foreseeable future."

Flash walked up and nuzzled her. "Oh and you too, Doggie. Did I tell you that you have a special file because you smelled out that Frontman? We now know dogs *hate* Squids and other aliens."

"When I'm eighteen, can I move out if I want to?" asked James.

"Yes," replied Camila. "Why you would I don't know."

"Just asking," James said.

"Anything else? Okay, let's eat. I'm hungry."

Later that night, Janice knocked on Camila's bedroom door.

"Come on in, Janice."

"If Matt and I want to get married... Can we?" Camila paused before she answered.

"You can if your guardian, me, signs off. Oh hell, in this day and age, I don't even know if that applies. The court system may be toast." She looked hard at Janice. "You're not...

"No, I'm not pregnant. Geesh, why does everyone jump to that conclusion? Like you said, in this day and age, tomorrow might not be here."

Camila sat on her bed and patted next to her. "Have a

seat, please." Janice sat next to here, and Camila put her arm around her. "We're family," the Sergeant said, "and thus we care for each other. If you love each other, to the exclusion of other possible mates, go for it. But remember your parents. It should be 'forever,' not just 'this week.'" Janice hugged Camila as she spoke.

"You're like the 'big sister' I never had."

"Question, Janice. Would you keep track of James, help him out if his... condition suddenly caused problems?"

"Of Course! He's my brother. And he'll be a great uncle when Matt and I have kids."

Camila looked at Janice. She felt this warmth in her heart and her gut that told her that there was a future if people like Janice and Matt planned to have kids, and take care of the family. She wondered if the Tschaaa had a family structure like this. Would that be a basis for a future understanding so they would stop attacking and eating humans? She could only hope.

"Okay. Keep us posted so someone can throw a wedding. Every woman needs one."

They hugged, and Janice left. Camila sat for a moment, then sighed. "I'm only twenty-five, and I already feel old. Damn."

17

Two days later. Camila, Torbin and USAF Master Sergeant Leroy Thompson were all sitting in a secure room in the Wing Headquarters Building. The room was secure to all known eavesdropping systems and to some supposed systems. Agent Leer had said initial analysis was that the Tschaaa had no real concept of OPSEC nor COMSEC as they did everything out in the open. They understood ambush hunting and long-range open surveillance as they had stupendous eyesight it seemed, but had no grasp of spy work, hacking, hidden listening devices, etcetera.

Camila looked at Agent Leer. "This plan definitely has your fingerprints all over it. I would have seen those even if Torbin had not told me."

"That is because," replied Leer, "you hold my abilities in such high regard."

This prompted a snort from Torbin.

"Okay," continued Leer. "Any questions?"

"Yeah," said Torbin. "We have the one Blackhawk. If

what or who we seize do not fit in the 'copter, what do we do? How do we get the 'package' home?"

"What did that Marine Gunny say?" answered Leer. "Improvise, adapt, overcome?"

"That was a movie," said Msgt. Thompson.

"Yes, but it fits this," replied Leer.

As they all rose to leave, Camila asked the Agent, "Can I talk to you about a personal matter?"

He frowned. "I guess, Sergeant."

Torbin and Leroy Thompson made themselves scarce.

"Here in this manila envelope are a bunch of papers about my wards. If something happens to me, I am asking you to help Matt ensure they have places to stay, educate, work, and just *live*. I question how stable our government is right now."

"And I should help because?" responded Leer.

"You like and use James and Janice. Down deep you have a heart. I know you do, as once in a while it gives off vibrations. So you'll take care of Emily. And Flash. Reasons enough?" Agent Leer looked at Camila. Then he took the envelope as he spoke.

"I don't tell people this, but somewhere out there in all this shit are my Wife, three kids, and an ex-wife and two kids. They are in areas overrun by Squids and their minions. I have not had contact with any of them since day two."

"Five kids? You don't look that old," interjected Camila.

"I started early. So, yes, I have a heart. And yes, I will help your wards out. But if you let it get out that I'm helping them, I will see to it that you are buried someplace in Antartica. Clear?"

Camila laughed as she answered, "Yes, Sir. Clear."

"Now get out of here before I change my mind."

After Camila left, Agent Leer opened the envelope and scanned the papers. He grunted.

"Daddy again and I didn't even get laid. Ain't that the shits."

Camila met Torbin and Leroy outside of the Wing HQ Building

"Things took care off?" asked Torbin.

"Yes, just had to arrange a few possibilities, thanks to my family I inherited along the way."

"I know that feeling," said Leroy, "but I made my kids with my wife, so no real surprise there."

"And I never had a wife nor kids. At least not that I know of."

"Hey, while I have you two alone," stated Leroy " let me tell you that I'm just a last minute add-on. This is your show." He looked at Camila. "I may have rank, but you know a helluva more about the enemy than I do. So as Ops NCO, you're Second in Command. I'm just a grunt."

"Master Sergeant, we younger PJs heard about you ages ago. And I read your After Action Report how you and your people extracted yourself from the Sand Box area and made it back here. No mean feat when everyone is shooting at everyone else."

"True. But you two fought the Squids and Company. With them, I'm a Cherry."

"Whatever," said Torbin. "Beer at the club?"

"Raincheck guys," said Camila. "I have to go see someone, then home."

"Okay. So I guess we wait until Leer says the balloon is going up, and what the final location will be."

"Roger that. Seeyas, Leroy, Torbin."

After she was out of earshot, Leroy said to Torbin," You two have something going on?"

"Kind of, sort of," answered Torbin. "I think we use each other for stress relief as neither of has had a so-called 'main squeeze' for a long while. Then the Squids showed up. My family was in San Diego. All gone now."

"I lucked out," replied Leroy. "My family was all in Fly

Over Country. So, some rocks, a few Deltas, a minimum of Harvester Arcs. So far that is." He gestured to Torbin. "Come on. First, six-pack is on me."

Camila knocked on the door to Lisa Tibbs' quarters. Lisa's silky voice called out. "Who is it?"

"A friend who is late getting back to you."

"Just a minute, Camila." A few moments later and Lisa undid the bolt and opened the door. She was wearing a kimono style robe that did little to conceal the curves underneath.

"Come on in, Camila. I'm just saying goodbye to my bunkmate, as I'll get my own quarters being an E-5."

Camila walked in and saw an attractive redhead woman Lisa's age and build, which meant she was cute and curvy. The redhead smiled as Camila saw the woman had a men's dress shirt on which was pulled up enough to see she had no panties on and a bottom to die for.

"I'm not interrupting anything…" Camila started to say when she was interrupted by Lisa shedding her robe.

"Heavens no, you're just in time for the party," Lisa said with a smile.

Three hours later and the party was just starting to wind down. Or was it? A nude Camila was laid across the redhead Sue's lap, also naked. Sue had a big grin on her face as she periodically spanked Camilas naturally tanned ass. Because Camila had her own panties shoved in her mouth, she could not verbalize any protests, if there were any. Instead, Camila produced some grunts and moans as she drooled a bit about her stuffed panties. Lisa had her hands trapped between her strong thighs, which did not matter as Camila had no desire to escape the 'torture.'

"You been a bad girl, you nasty little bitch," Lisa purred at the 'captive.' "We are just going to discipline this out of you, you slut you."

Sue smacked Camila's ass then slid a fingertip between

Camila's bodacious ass cheeks. The PJs eyes widened just as Lisa released the captive's hands, yanked the panties from her mouth and forced her tongue into it.

There was an explosion with did not involve any gunpowder or plastic explosives.

As Lisa put Camila's bra back on for her and nuzzled her neck, the PJ looked down and noticed her own nipples were covered with lipstick and gloss. Camila then felt what could only be a tongue exploring an area her panties were about to conceal. She moaned, grabbed two handfuls of Sue's red hair and guided her towards nirvana.

Camila made it home before the Witching Hour. As she went into her room, Janice came to her door. She looked at Camila and smirked.

"You have a couple hickeys on your neck," said Janice. "Rough night with a certain male Marine?"

"Tobin's too much of a gentleman to try and 'mark' his territory, " Camila replied. "let's just say I may not be 'confused' anymore."

Janice giggled, then followed Camila into her room.

"May I ask a personal question?"

"Shoot, Janice."

"If both sexes, genders, can turn you on, how do you figure out the whole love thing?"

Camila looked at Janice. She kept forgetting that Janice was still a teenager with limited experience with human relationships, despite being involved with shooting and killing of both humans and aliens.

"Love is... love. Sex can express your love if done right. When you love someone, things usually... click. When you love, you yearn for their smell, touch, voice, sight, just their presence beside you. But even then, you have to work to keep that love. Otherwise, it can fade."

"You have loved someone like that?" Janice asked.

"Yes. And to head off the next question, of both genders. And to be a bit crude about physical attributes at your age, both genitalia has their own special taste, touch, and feel. But again, that is the physical part. Its what it creates in your gut and your heart that matters."

Janice paused in thought for a few moments, then sat on the bed next Camila. "We are not related, so what stopped you from being attracted to me?"

"Moral upbringing that says some things are not right and should not be done as it usually screws things up, Janice. Just remember that when you are raising your kids with Matt. Like I said before, you should know Matt is the one. Please don't think there are 'do-overs' like in video games."

"Camila, you never found Miss or Mister Right?"

The Sergeant shrugged, then replied. "Thought I had. But my job gets in the way. Especially when you are female, and you are doing a nasty, physical job. People still have trouble with women doing those types of jobs. We can give life through our wombs. So some people think we are doing things wrong when we become takers of life. Men are traditionally seen as built more to be the takers of life. They are bigger, with stronger muscles on average to handle weapons." Camila chuckled. "Then Colonel Colt and Company came along and really screwed things up."

"What?" asked Janice.

"God created humankind. Colonel Colt and his pistols made them all equal. A one hundred pound woman can stop a two hundred pound rapist with a well placed twenty-two caliber bullet. Powered through the energy and chemistry of gunpowder."

"You think the Tschaaa coming may change all we know about men and women?" asked Janice.

"Last answer, Janice. I need sleep. We women may have to step up more, be more nasty, violent. I hope that does not change who we really are. Givers of life."

Janice rose off the bed, then hugged Camila. "Thanks for helping save James and me, Camila. Thanks for being 'you' when we all need help. Good Night."

"Good night. Sweet dreams with Matt, Janice."

"Of course," replied Janice with a small chuckle.

After Camila had dressed for bed, which included a man's old dress shirt—that was so damned sexy with Sue and her butt—she lay down and for the first time in weeks, said a little prayer.

"Lord, help all these young ones to grow and persevere. It was bad enough when I was growing up around the Barrio. Now they have Bug-Eyed Monsters trying to eat them. Help us. In Jesus name, Amen."

The balloon went up a week later. Agent Leeds contacted those involved that James' unique analysis had found some Tschaaa activities which pointed to an unusual target. The Hanford Nuclear Explosion had contaminated much of Lower Eastern Washington State and vast chunks of Idaho, on over to the far west of Montana and up into Canada. The prevailing winds had led to the severe fall out to be blown east by north east, up towards Spokane. Thus it was probably just as well that Fairchild Air Force Base had been trashed and abandoned before that. However, using satellite imagery and some limited drones—the Tschaaa had kept many of the satellites for their own use, yet lacked the idea that humans could still hack into them and use them also—James Richards had seen some photos of some unusual activity. Apparently, within 48 hours of the invasion, a group of Tschaaa had started swimming up the Columbia River, and into the interior. Thus they had also infested the Snake and Spokane Rivers which led to the ambush attack on so-called 'Richards

Raiders.'

James had noticed something in the analysis. There seemed to be two different groups. The first ones were smatterings of what James called Young Scout Warriors, doing the work for what humans thought were a form "Lord," Senior Tschaaa that ran everything through their offspring. They were young bucks trying to prove their mettle. But following part way up the Columbia behind them was a bunch of smaller groups. It took a while to figure out they were females with young. A river the size of the Columbia not only provided good food sources in the form of both fish and humans lining the banks in towns, but they also offered bodies of water devoid of any unknown large ocean or water predator. And in September, the water had still been warm. Even in October, it was not difficult to provide heated areas the Tschaaa young, and alleged gavid females seemed to prefer. Crash courses in Tschaaa culture pointed to there being an attempt at a breeding colony in the Columbia. Nuclear Contamination was screwing that plan up once the Squids realized the contaminants were being dispersed in the waters *and* the air. Now there was a scramble to get all Tschaaa away from any contamination and back down towards Portland, Oregon, which had become a hub of activity thanks to its proximity to the Pacific Ocean and a primary river system, rumblings of Mount St. Helens and Ranier are notwithstanding.

The plan was to sneak up by the Columbia while Sqds were rushing to an fro in a bit of a panic (just how dangerous they were about their Young would be figured out at a later date) and grab a 'less aggressive' Female and some more manageable.

Camila tried to sneak out in the middle of the night with her gear and leave a note behind. She had forgotten. However, James had all the details as he was a primary author of the Intelligence behind the Operations Plan. She did not even reach the front door.

"Where do you think you're going?" Matt caught her at the door. Coming from the rest of the rooms were her Family.

"I am going to work. I have to leave now. And its classified so don't ask for details…"

Emily walked up and hugged her, kissed her, then stepped back. "You be careful, Aunt Cammy."

Sergeant Sanchez, lifetaker and heartbreaker, began to stutter. Then one by one, James, Janice, and Matt came up and did the same. Camila tried to stop her own tears but was unsuccessful. Even Flash the Greyhound came up and gave her a wet kiss.

"All we wanted to do was to say 'see you later' and tell you we love you, Camila," explained Janice. "We know you have to do this. It's your job. But at least let us say how much we love and appreciate all you have done."

"And we will be here when you get back," said James. "Unlike other people in your past."

"Somebody has been snooping where they shouldn't have been," scolded Camila.

"Please be quiet," instructed James, "and come here for a group hug."

A picture of the 'group hug' was somehow taken and archived, to be of importance later. Camila finally was able to detach herself and headed towards the flight line. There were a whole bunch of stops, twists and turned between Malmstrom and a spot on the Columbia River.

TSGT Camila Sanchez sat between Master Gunnery Sergeant Torbin Bender and the more massive USAF Master Sergeant on the Blackhawk Helicopter. As they sat awaiting clearance to their first refueling point, Torbin pointed out something sticking out from one of her pockets. Camila pulled the object out. It was a handmade a card from Emily.

"From Your Brood to our Surrogate Mother Hen. Thanks for Keeping us Chicks Safe. See you soon." It was signed by all, including a noseprint from Flash the Greyhound. Camila tried not to weep, but Torbin gave her a very ragged handkerchief.

"Ain't family grand?" he said.

"Smartass," Camila said.

"No. Just jealous. Always remember. Family makes this," the Marine swept his arm to be all-inclusive, "worthwhile. And don't you forget it."

"Wise man there," said Leroy, "for a Jarhead,"

"Get bent, prophead."

Camila began to laugh.

"COVERING FIRE!" someone yelled out as the nine-person unit tried to fight its way out of a significant FUBAR and Mongolian Goat Rope. Like humans, female Tschaaa could be warriors also. Unlike human babies, Tschaaa young develop quickly, being highly mobile in water by the end of the first year. And eight arms and two social tentacles with five digit hands on the end were strong, especially in full-grown adult Tschaaa.

The humans also found out that the Squids could communicate for miles underwater with no artificial devices, just with their voices, as whales can. When the unit tried to grab the Young Squid sunning itself on the shore as it examined some Earth sea creature shells, the action had been seen by a Creche mate. The alarm was almost instantaneous. A Breeder showed up and instantly attacked, moving almost crablike on land. Then another, then another female. Even with just crude blade weapons, they threw themselves at the humans, who cut them down with their firearms.

Then the males and Harvester Robots showed up.

Camila was on automatic, shooting and reloading as targets presented themselves. She had done this before, knew that bullets did a number on Squids if you hit them in the right place. The same with the Six Wheeled Robots. However, you have to have enough bullets.

"Dust Off is Down! Dust Off is Down!" Something or someone had gotten to the Blackhawk. They had killed a couple of human renegades also so some traitor may have sounded the alarm about the helicopter.

"We need transport," Torbin yelled over the radio.

"Any land vehicle," Camila called out. "Get away from the water and into the trees. Then all you have to worry about are the Deltas and Robots."

"What about the Robocops?" someone called out.

"Just deal with it!"

"I've got the Rear!" Camila yelled out as she lit up a fast-moving shape that was a Harvester Rob. It spat sparks and began to belch black smoke. She tossed a grenade and hot-footed to the next piece of cover.

Things went black.

Not for the first time did Torbin Bender and Leroy Thompson limp from a Memorial Service. The group who joked about being Camila's "brood" showed up, as did a bunch more people she had touched, including a Staff Sergeant Lisa Gibbs and a Special Agent John Leer. Four others had died, but Camila Sanchez was Missing in Action. With human eating creatures, it made the condition worse.

Torbin noticed that James Richard did not seem all that upset. He knew about James "condition" that supposedly manifested itself at the most inopportune times and places. So Torbin Bender, being the nosey smartass he was, walked up to James.

"Hey, buddy, how are you doing?"

"You are wondering why I am nor bawling my eyes out," challenged James.

"Hey. People deal with grief—"

"Read this, and then keep quiet."

Torbin was not used to being ordered about by young and strange civilians, but given the circumstances, he went along with it. He looked at the message.

"Well, I'll be damned."

RECORDED UNKNOWN SPEAKER.

"Yeah, the Squids said to keep her alive, said they wanted to examine a breedable female warrior. Not for eating. Ain't that the shits?"

Torbin looked at James. "Who knows this?"

"You do now, Torbin Bender. And you also know this. "Where there is life, there is hope."

www.ingramcontent.com/pod-product-compliance
Lightning Source LLC
Chambersburg PA
CBHW070540100726
47907CB00004B/1200